city girls

city girls

a novel

loretta lopez

TRIANGLE
SQUARE
books for young readers

SEVEN STORIES PRESS
New York / Oakland / London

SEVEN STORIES PRESS
140 Watts Street
New York, NY 10013
www.sevenstories.com

LIBRARY OF CONGRESS CATALOGING-IN-PUBLICATION DATA

Names: Lopez, Loretta, author.
Title: City girls / Loretta Lopez.
Description: New York : Triangle Square Books for Young Readers / Seven
    Stories Press, 2024. | Audience: Ages 10-14 years. | Audience: Grades
    7-9.
Identifiers: LCCN 2023034142 | ISBN 9781644213421 (hardcover) | ISBN
    9781644213438 (ebook)
Subjects: CYAC: Friendship--Fiction. | Family life--Fiction. | Middle
    schools--Fiction. | Schools--Fiction. | New York (N.Y.)--Fiction. |
    LCGFT: Novels.
Classification: LCC PZ7.1.L66785 Ci 2024 | DDC [E]--dc23
LC record available at https://lccn.loc.gov/2023034142

College professors and high school and middle school teachers may order free examination copies of Seven Stories Press titles. Visit https://www.sevenstories.com/pg/resources-academics or email academic@sevenstories.com.

Printed in the United States of America

9 8 7 6 5 4 3 2 1

Elisa

1

My body is still getting used to hers. And even though I don't want to, I flinch as my mami runs her fingers through my black hair. I don't really know what she thinks of me yet, but she does say my hair is as smooth as rose petals. I wish she would tell me that I'm beautiful, or that she missed me a lot, or that I'm really smart. I know Ms. Lee and Ms. Luz think I'm smart, but they also think I'm annoying. They narrow their eyes when I can't stop fidgeting, when I make drawings of them, when I laugh out loud while they talk and talk.

On the subway, I look at the other girls. From a distance they don't seem too different from me. Maybe they're also smart and annoying. Maybe their hair is also soft. Maybe their mamis also don't tell them that they are beautiful. But do they feel what I'm feeling? That all of this seems impossible? I try to imagine their thoughts. Are they remembering something? What are they remembering? Do their memories feel like mine, like foggy stories, like dreams?

2

Everything is new: new city, new house, new school. It's almost like my mami is new too because we haven't seen each other in a very long time. She left when I was four, so that makes it seven whole years. Now we spend so much time together. Every morning we take a really long subway ride to my new school on the Upper West Side of Manhattan, NYC. My mami says it's worth it because it's a nice school in a nice neighborhood (I guess that means our neighborhood is not nice). My mami says it's also lucky I got here in September so I could start with the other kids who have been here all along. Everything feels fast and gigantic, ready to pop and burst into sparks. My mami says she used to feel like that too but not anymore.

We are in front of the school. I look at the other kids and they aren't holding their moms' hands the way I am. A lot of them come alone, they just walk in like it's nothing. My mami kisses me on the forehead and whispers, "Be good, hermosa." I go into the enormous brown building with lots of windows like eyes and stairs like teeth. I give everyone pretty smiles because that's what my mami would like. She wants everyone to think I'm cute. She says they will treat me better if they think that.

Before class starts, I practice names. There's Lola, Francesca, Julio, Aisha, Tobias, Lobo (which is a weird thing to name your kid, if you ask me—no one would name their kid "Wolf" in El Salvador), Alice, and Lucia. Soon I find out that Lola is the popular girl. She wears beautiful dresses and skirts that fit her perfectly. She likes light pink and white. They match her long blond hair. Everyone thinks she looks like an angel and wishes she acted like one because she says the meanest things that stick in your brain for a long time. Alice is the opposite of Lola. She likes black and dark pink. She cuts her hair like a boy. She doesn't sit up straight. She bends over her drawings that come one after the other. Lots of people think her drawings are gross and weird but I think they're funny. Yesterday she drew Mr. Mack with a rat face. Lucia is the only other kid who knows how to actually speak Spanish. She also has long black hair and light brown skin like me. But she's not from El Salvador. She's from Mexico but maybe she's just a little bit from Mexico because she said she was born in NYC. Lucia is shy but seems to like me. Maybe she wants to be my friend. I don't know if that's a good idea because Lucia's actually a nice girl and I'm just pretending.

3

After school, my mami takes me downtown to Leah's office. Right before we go in, she puts my hair in the highest ponytail and tells me to stand up straight. She tells me to be on my best behavior because we both need Leah, need her more than anyone, because I am an illegal person. Leah has the bluest eyes I have ever seen. Sometimes when she's talking, I stop listening and I think of an ocean the color of her eyes and I think of myself swimming in it and then I think of diving in deep. Really deep. Under a rock I find something secret: the gold crown of a dead queen. I want to carry it up to the surface and put it on my mami's head.

"Elisa," she asks, "where were you born?"

I was born in El Salvador whose colors are white and blue.

And now I'm here in America whose colors are red, white, and blue. Americans like these three colors. They flap outside of houses and buildings, people put them on their cars and inside of stores and schools. It's like they are worried they will forget where they are if they don't see the colors. In El Salvador, we knew where we were. We couldn't forget.

Leah tells me my memories are "essential." She is going to use them to build up her case, my case, of why I should stay in the United States. My mami tells me to tell Leah *everything*. She says the more I tell her the better chance we have of staying together. She says, *don't lie, Elisa*. If I lie, they might send me away, back to San Marcos, with my abuela.

"Elisa," Leah says. "Tell me about El Salvador. What was it like living with your grandma?"

My mami sits next me. I look at her for answers but her eyes tell me she doesn't know. We spent a long time apart. I just got here. My mami has been living in America without me. First in Texas, then in North Carolina, and now, in New York. She says we are getting to know each other all over again.

Leah looks into my eyes. She has a sweet smile. I can tell my silence makes her a little worried. I'm trying to find an answer for her but when I look into her blue eyes, I leave my body to swim away into a clear ocean. Maybe if I go there, I won't feel like the words coming out of me are actually mine.

4

Some days I can talk to Leah about my memories. To make it easier she gives me paper and markers. My mami told her I like to draw, or actually she told the lady who translates her Spanish into English that I like to draw. In Leah's office, I hear everything my mami says twice because I can speak both languages. I learned English without even trying when I was in that orphanage in Texas. It was only a month that they kept me before giving me to Mami, but it felt like years. Years of feeling all the new words in my mouth. They kept coming and coming.

Leah says, "Can you draw your house back in El Salvador?"

I draw a blue house. I draw the three dogs outside of it. I miss them. They were always outside even though I wanted them inside. I tell my lawyer this. I feel it's important, more than the blue house and my abuela inside of it. I draw her behind a window.

"Who's that?" asks my lawyer, pointing to my abuela. I made her really small so that she wouldn't notice her. "Tell me about her."

I tell it like a story because people like stories and I like Leah: "Once upon a time, there was an abuela. Some days she was nice and other days she was very mean."

My lawyer's eyes turn bright. This is the look she gives me when I have to say more for her to write down. She told me she's going to give everything she writes to an officer. Then, the officer will read it and interview me. That officer will give all his notes to his boss and they will decide if I can stay.

I draw a dog that's bigger than the blue house. It has huge pointy teeth and laser eyes. It has the power to zap and freeze my abuela. Then she stops hitting me. I start laughing. Leah asks me about the dog. I want to tell her about its magical power but I don't.

After the meeting my mami buys me a hamburger and French fries, which I love. The food is so salty and delicious in my mouth it gets rid of the empty feeling I usually get after talking about El Salvador. As I eat, my mami reminds me that I have to talk about the ugly things that happened for a reason. She says that America lets kids stay in the country if terrible things happened to them somewhere else. She says I should feel grateful America is giving me a chance and I should give them everything they need. But I don't feel very grateful, and I am still hungry. My mami buys me an ice cream at the counter. I wait for her at the table, I lick my finger, and pick up little bits of salt. They look like the tiniest diamonds.

A lady sits at the table next to mine. She is talking on the phone very loud and her voice takes me out of my tiny diamonds. She has the longest nails I've ever seen, purple and shiny. Later, after I eat my ice cream and we take the subway home, I make two drawings: one of the lady with the purple nails and another of a rat I saw on the subway tracks. When my mami looks at them her eyebrows get closer together and she nibbles on her lower lip. Then she puts her hand on her stomach where a baby is growing.

I think my drawings confuse my mami. She is never sure if she likes them but she keeps them all in a nice pink box. Sometimes when I draw things like the sun, or a flower, or Kitty sleeping, she puts the drawing on the fridge. This makes my body feel tingly and light. I wish I could make more pretty drawings but I think they're boring and that's not what comes out onto the paper.

5

When my mami wakes me up this morning I see anger in her eyes. *Wake up, hurry up, let's go . . .* she keeps saying in a mean tone. I try to think if I did anything bad, but I can't think of anything.

"Mami, what's wrong?" I ask. She stops and looks at me. Really looks at me. I see her eyes are puffy. Suddenly the anger floats away from her and now all that's left is sadness. My mami puts her hand on her forehead.

"Nothing is wrong, mi amor," she says. "I'm sorry. It's nothing. Sometimes I just get into a dark mood."

On the walk from the subway to school we are quiet. I like the feeling of my hand in hers. She has soft hands and long fingers. Everything about my mami is lovely: her walk, her smooth hair, her honey-colored catlike eyes. I really do love her even when she gets angry and sad and confused. I think my mami loves me too. If not, she would have never asked for me to come. She would have just let me stay in the blue house in San Marcos forever.

6

At school I'm drawing the playground at the orphanage. I'm coloring in the big blueish green cactus growing on the other side of the fence, the stupidly hot yellow slide that burned our legs, and for some reason my dogs are there. They have sharp teeth and spiky collars like the one Alice is wearing. When they growl the earth beneath the orphanage rumbles.

In the next drawing, I will make sure the earth splits open and swallows us all.

All of a sudden I feel a soft thud on my arm. It's a piece of paper folded into a tiny neat square. I look behind me but no one is looking. I open it.

To: Elisa
From: Lucia
I like your drawing. ☺

I think it would be rude not to respond. So, I turn the little paper and write as neat as I can:

Thank you. Do you like to draw?

When Ms. Lee turns around, I throw it to Lucia's desk and it lands perfect right in the middle and she smiles back at me. We do that all class back and forth. Back and forth.

7

after school, Leah asks me about my abuela again. My mami glares at me with her cat eyes. So even though my tongue and my chest and my belly don't want to, I say it. I tell Leah about the time she hit me with a belt, the time she whipped me with her cellphone cord, the time she hit me with a broom, another time when she threw a hot pan at me, and then there was the time she tied me to a pole. The dogs barked and barked at her and I barked too until she slapped me across the face. My mami winces and touches her cheek like if someone just slapped her. I don't like to talk about things that make my mami hurt.

Afterwards on the subway, my mami tells me something

she has already told me before. I think this time she's saying it more to herself than to me.

"Elisa," she says in a low voice. She's stroking my hair with her lovely hands. "I didn't want to leave you with your abuela. I *had* to do it. There were men in San Marcos that wanted me dead. I had to run away and I couldn't take you with me. You were too little. You would have died on the trip. I came here to work and send you money. I wanted you to have a better life. I never thought things would be so horrible for you."

I look at another little girl sitting in the orange seat across from me. She has skin as dark as the night and her hair is in a hundred braids tied up with gold bands and beads. Her mami is the bigger version of her. They are both beautiful. I imagine they are a princess and a queen that live in the tallest building in NYC. Every night they look down at the sad people on the street and send them mother-daughter love through their magic eyes. The mother raises her eyebrows and shoots her love at Mami. She wipes away all her dark moods and makes her mind shiny and bright.

"It's OK, Mami," I say, squishing her hand as hard as I can.

8

Today I feel a little icky. Maybe I have one of my mami's dark moods . . . If mothers can pass the color of their eyes to their kids, why couldn't they pass on a dark mood? Maybe abuela passed it on to my mami and my mami passed it on to me. It lives inside of us like a tiny little black ball and then sometimes it breaks and spills all over.

Lucia sends me a note. It says: *What are you drawing?*

I look down at my notebook. I have made the shape of a man but you can't see his face. He is behind a red cloud. I realize that I don't know what I'm drawing but I know it's something disgusting and I don't want to tell Lucia anything about it. My drawing makes my heart speed up. My dark mood has turned into thick liquid and I'm starting to drown in it. I can't breathe. I can't stay in the classroom. I leave without permission. I need to be somewhere alone. Somewhere cool. The bathroom. I'm splashing cold water on my face. I feel a tiny bit better but still horrible. All I can do is lock myself in a stall and sit on the toilet. Wait until it ends.

Someone walks in. I recognize Ms. Luz's blue flats and brown feet. She knocks very softly on the stall.

"What's wrong, sweetie?" she asks. "Are you sick?"

I open the door and nod because I know I need help and Ms. Luz is nice. She has a big strong body and a warm voice.

She gives me her hand and we walk together to the nurse. By the time we arrive to the nurse I feel a little better. I tell Ms. Luz and the nurse I feel all better and not to call my mami because they would only make her worry and that women with babies in their stomach need to stay calm. But they don't listen. I wait for her on one of those hard beds in between two thin ugly curtains and fall asleep. My mami wakes me up. She looks beautiful, wearing her gold earrings and a gold necklace. Her belly looks perfectly round. I think about my baby brother. It is good he will be born here and that he will never have to hate and love and miss El Salvador all at the same time like I do. He won't think about the awful people and the wonderful people in the blue and pink houses, the parties in the streets, a loud scary sound in the dark, the mountains looking down at us, the stray dogs howling at the sky.

I pretend to fall back asleep when my mami and the nurse are talking. They speak in Spanish. The nurse says she thinks I had an ataque de pánico. She asks my mami if I see a therapist. My mami says no. She tells the nurse that she wants me to be normal and happy and that normal and happy children don't see therapists. She says, "Talking more about the past is not going to help." The nurse disagrees. She tells my mami that whatever happened in El Salvador needs to be processed, let out of my body. Then she says, "It's hard to deal with Elisa all by yourself."

My mami sighs loud. She's annoyed at the nurse. She opens the curtain roughly. I feel like I'm in trouble and I'm angry at the nurse and Ms. Luz for calling my mami when I told them not to. We leave the school without talking and walk into the chilly sunshine. My mami says we should buy ourselves a treat. She takes me to a fancy shop with cookies, cakes, and cupcakes every single color of the rainbow. I chose a cupcake with pink frosting and sprinkles.

"Oh, wow! Qué cute," says my mami trying to use her English. She wants us to be cheerful so I give her a smile but really, I think the cupcake is gross. Part of me wants to smash it with my tennis shoes. I control myself because if I did that then my mami would really think I'm crazy. I ask my mami for water and I drink a whole bottle on my own very fast. Then I eat the ugly cupcake.

9

Back home, in the kitchen, my mami makes pupusas. She doesn't ask me about el ataque de pánico at all. Instead, she tells me to rest. She gives me her phone so I can play games and watch videos. I don't complain.

My mami makes dinner for Octavio and me every evening. Octavio lives with us or maybe we live with Octavio. Sometimes when we are walking around Manhattan my mami points up at a building that touches the sky and says, "Octavio made that." I believe her because Octavio is big and strong and he comes back to the apartment covered in dust and paint. When my mami sees him walk into the apartment her eyes get big. She tells me I should be very grateful for Octavio. Octavio pays for my food, my clothes, my books for school, my colored pencils, everything. One time, after Octavio bought me a toy at a street fair my mami said I should be nicer to him. I said, "Why? I didn't ask him to buy it for me."

Her eyes got narrow and scary. She said, "I didn't raise you to be a spoiled brat." After that I tried to be a little nicer to Octavio because I want her to be happy.

Octavio only looks at my mami and her belly when we eat dinner together. They talk about their days and they don't ask me about mine. When I'm especially bored, I interrupt their grown-up talk and tell them a crazy story. I'll say something like: did you ever hear about what happened to the baby who drove her car to Mexico? And some days my mami will say "Shht, Elisa, don't be rude," and other days the two of them will listen for a while. I can't wait to have a baby brother to play with. I know he will like my stories and ask me questions.

My mami told me he has three more months to grow inside her belly and that seems like a long time for a baby to swim in the dark.

10

Right before we leave the house for school, I get a stomachache. I say, "Mami, I can't go to school. My stomach hurts." My mami rolls her eyes like she doesn't believe me and I get super mad. "Mami!" I yell. "I'm telling the truth!"

"Stop it," she says in her scary voice that cuts into my brain like a sharp knife. "You are not a sick little girl. First this nonsense from yesterday and now this? You are going to school."

I can't help it and tears fall down my face. My mami pretends that they are not even there. She takes my hand and we walk out of the building. On the subway my stomachache doesn't stop and it gets even worse but I'm too afraid of mami's sharp voice and say nothing. I start to think about how I must have really looked weird yesterday running out of the classroom like that. I also think about Lucia's note and how I never answered it and how she probably thinks I'm crazy. I hold my stomach and my mami takes out her phone and starts to play a sparkly game. I think, *I hate you.* But I know deep, deep down in my heart that it's not true. I know she could have ignored me forever and left me in El Salvador forever, and even then I would still love her.

11

ight when I walk into the classroom the girl named Alice runs up to Julio's desk and puts her wet finger into his ear. Julio is the prettiest boy in the class and we all like him.

"YUCK!" Julio shrieks and he holds his ear as if it were bleeding.

Alice starts laughing like a little devil, showing her sharp teeth. Everyone else is saying, *ewwwww, gross! Alice is such a freak.* No one is even looking at me and no one cares at all about me running out of the classroom yesterday. I decide that I like freaky Alice. A lot. At recess, I decide to hang out with her instead of Lucia. Lucia's eyes get big and hurt and I try to pretend I don't see them. Alice and I play basketball with the boys and we run and shout and bump into them on purpose. Alice says big swear words and I do too for the first time. They make us laugh and laugh. The boys smell horrible and we make fun of them and laugh some more. Lobo gets very annoyed at Alice and crashes into her hard. She falls and scrapes her knee and rips her hot pink tights. Alice doesn't care at all. She gets right back up.

12

fter school, my mami and I go to Leah's office. I can tell my mami is tired going up and down the dirty subway stairs with my baby brother inside her. I feel bad because if I weren't here, she wouldn't have to do it.

In the office, Leah says I need to talk to a psychologist about what happened to me in El Salvador. The psychologist will write a letter to the judge about how I should stay in America with Mami. But I really don't feel like talking to a new person.

I say, "Isn't that what you're already doing for me?" My mami's eyes turn into sharp arrows.

Leah explains in her gentle voice that she is a lawyer and a psychologist's letter can make our case extra strong. It will be more evidence from another expert. Leah says I only need to see the psychologist once. My mami seems to relax a little when she hears this. Still, on the subway she pinches my ear. She tells me to never talk back to Leah who is being so nice to us, Leah who is doing all of this for free. I feel bad and my eyes fill up with tears that don't fall.

13

"What happened to you the other day?" Lucia asks at recess.

I act like I don't know what she's talking about but Lucia is smarter than me.

"The day you ran out of class," Lucia says, "after I sent you the note, what happened?"

I like Lucia's face. Everything is small and her eyes are big and sparkly.

"I think it's called a panic attack," I say and the words coming out of my mouth surprise me because I wasn't sure what happened to me. But now I know. Lucia starts talking about how I should see a psychologist or a social worker because they can help with panic attacks. Lucia knows about it because her mom is a doctor. She talks about it like it's nothing bad or horrible, just something that happened. I tell her a little more.

"I'm going to a psychologist . . . but for something different."

I end up telling Lucia a lot but not everything. I tell her that I'm trying to get asylum to stay in the United States. I tell her that the psychologist needs to write a letter to the judge that says I can't go back to El Salvador because if I do, I might go crazy or die. I tell her that if I get to stay, I might not be able to go back to El Salvador ever again.

My life sounds like an interesting story when I tell it to Lucia. She can't believe that I secretly crossed three countries with people who were strangers at first but not at the end. She can't believe they took me to a jail and then to an orphanage. She can't believe that it might have all been for nothing and I could get sent back. She can't believe that if I stay, I might never see El Salvador again. It makes her so sad and angry. She starts to tell me a little bit about Mexico. How her abuela lives there and how she loves Mexico very much. Then she stops. I think she doesn't know if that was the right thing to say. I take my sandwich and stuff a huge piece in my mouth so that I don't have to talk. My throat feels too thick. I gulp my orange juice while Lucia tries to understand my life.

14

I skip school so that my mami can take me to the psychologist's office. My stomach feels squirmy. I would rather curl up with Kitty on the couch at home and not move. But I see the darkness in my mami's eyes and I don't want her to pinch my ear again so I let her comb my hair into braids.

I feel a little better when I see the office. The psychologist's name is Jackie and she's a nice old lady with long silver hair. She speaks Spanish and says that all we are going to do today is play. Jackie tells my mami she can come look at the room but that then she has to sit outside. Jackie shows us all of her things. She has books, puzzles, colors, paints, dolls, stuffed animals, puppets, playdoh . . . Once my mami leaves she asks me if I want to use anything. I point at the box of dolls. I feel a little embarrassed because I think I'm too old for dolls—eleven-year-olds don't play with them. But Jackie says, "Nice choice!" We sit on a green carpet. My favorite is the doll with the blue eyes and the brown long hair because I think she looks like Leah. Jackie asks me why I chose her and I say, "Because she is the prettiest." She smiles and scribbles something on her yellow notepad. Jackie chooses a doll with brown skin and black hair. I don't say anything.

The dolls live in a cottage inside a forest. Even though she is a grown-up, Jackie is good at playing. When I tell her, she laughs and writes something else on her notepad. The dolls have a pretty nice life. They eat berries, they live in a cozy cabin, they are friends with the deer and rabbits, and they swim in a lake every day. My doll is named Isabel and Jackie's doll is named Nina. Since they are best friends, they tell each other everything.

One day after swimming Isabel says, "You know, I have some ugly secrets. They are so ugly I don't even tell my mami."

Nina replies, "It must be hard keeping those secrets all to yourself."

Isabel shrugs. She eats a delicious red berry from her basket. "I'm a strong and brave girl. I can keep my secrets all to myself."

Jackie looks at me straight in the eyes and says, "There are lots of ways girls can be strong. Sometimes talking about horrible things is the bravest thing a girl can do."

I throw Isabel across the room. I feel red and hot.

"I'm bored of dolls," I say.

Jackie and I sit at a small table and make animals out of playdough. I'm very good at this and I start to feel less annoyed at her and her office. I make Kitty, curled up and sleeping. Then I smash her and turn her into a lion. We say goodbye. My mami buys me pizza for being a good girl. I don't tell her I threw Isabel across the room.

Everything is OK until later that night. I dream of a red curtain. Behind the red curtain my drawing appears, the one that made me run outside the classroom. My drawing starts off fuzzy but becomes clearer and clearer and then I can see him, really see him, the man who hurt me. He wears a crown and is the king like he said he was. The crown is made of chicken bones. Back in El Salvador, he liked to eat chicken next to my abuela. They would both lick their fingers. The dream is filled with their sucking sounds. In the dream, he can hear the words in my head. He can feel that I want to say what he did. But I won't say it. He has a knife to put into my mami's heart. It's shining there in the dark.

"Mami!" I yell and she comes into the room. She's in her white pajamas and she has her hair down. She looks like an angel. She kisses my wet face and tells me it was just a nightmare. She doesn't ask me what it was about. My mami doesn't want to know about the things in my head.

15

I think about the man a lot. I don't want to, but I do. He's standing behind the red curtain in my brain and whenever he wants to, he pops out from behind it with a sticky finger on his mouth saying, *shhhhhh.* Sometimes he wears the chicken bone crown and a black suit. Other times he's wearing his disguise: a normal t-shirt and jeans. These were the clothes he wore when he fixed the door, a crack in the ceiling, a faucet. He always made abuela happy.

The next time I am in Leah's office I feel like he is behind her desk, curled up, listening. I know this isn't true because he is in San Marcos, but I walk over just to make sure.

"Ay, Elisa!" says my mami. "What are you doing? Sit down."

I feel better knowing he's not there but I still don't want to talk. Leah knows it. She puts her pen down. I tell my mami I'm hungry and thirsty. The translator says she can bring me some chips and a juice box. My mami rolls her eyes. "You just ate," she says. "You are going to get fat." I'm a little worried about getting fat but I say, "Pleaaaaseeeeee." I eat all the chips and drink all the juice. Then I have to go to the bathroom. I take an extra-long time. When I come back it is time to go home. On the subway, I can tell my mami is annoyed at me. She doesn't talk. She puts her hands on her belly and keeps her eyes closed all the way home.

16

I think about the chicken man at school. Sometimes when I go to the bathroom alone during class, I'm pretty sure that I'm going to find him there standing on the pink tile, so I turn right back around and hold it until Lucia can come with me. He won't hurt me if I'm with someone else. He never did.

At lunch, I get nervous all of a sudden. I hear Alice start to argue with Lobo. They are sitting at the table next to ours. They're talking about a game. Something about how to kill someone better, quicker. "Assault rifle!" Lobo shouts. "Sniper gun!" Alice yells back. Her cheeks are getting red and Lobo is laughing at her. I feel like the chicken man is going to walk through the cafeteria doors with a machete in his hand. He's going to come and take me away forever. I push my fingernail into my arm deep, deeper, so that it hurts. Lucia whispers into my ear, "What are you doing?" She grabs my hand and holds it tight. I squeeze back hard.

17

The chicken man likes it best when I am alone in bed at night. Then he can come out from behind the curtains and remind me about our secrets. I try to think of school, of Kitty, of my new baby brother, but he's a big man and he takes up all of my brain.

One night when he is not letting me sleep, I tiptoe into the kitchen and find a box of cookies. They are my favorite crunchy, extra-sweet, chocolate cookies. I put a whole one into my mouth. I pretend the *crunch, crunch, crunch,* is me turning him into dust. I keep eating until my stomach feels like it is ready to pop. Then I wobble back into bed and, even though my belly hurts, I fall asleep.

The next night he's there again, behind my eyes. He's sitting on a throne made of chicken bones. I remember him and my abuela killing chickens in the patio with a machete. They held the chicken upside down by the feet and cut the throat. The blood fed the lime trees. I thought the man and my abuela were brave when they did that. I had to close my eyes but they kept theirs open the whole time.

Now I open my eyes. I'm in the dark. I get up to go to the fridge. Its bright light and the cold air make me feel a little better. I see the red and purple juice boxes my mami has lined up for me to take to school. She hates it when I drink them at home because she says they are expensive. I take one anyway. If I drink enough sweet juice maybe I will drown the man who lives inside my body. Then he will disappear and I won't remember him. I take one juice box and then another one. I drink every last drop, I crush the boxes, and throw them on the floor. For a long time, I don't realize my mami is standing in the hallway watching me in her cat-like way—silent and still.

"Elisa," she says in a small voice. I take a few steps back because I am afraid she will hit me for being bad. But she is not angry, she is sad. We are looking at each other. We stay like that for a long time, quiet. Then she does something I have never seen her do before. She sits on the floor in the dark hallway. Her back is against the wall and her legs are crossed. "Come," she says. I go over. She's looking up at me. She looks so small, so pretty. I feel gigantic and disgusting.

She asks, "What happened in San Marcos?" I look away, but she tugs on my wrist and says, "Besides abuela, who else hurt you?"

I try to pull away from her but she's much stronger than me. I fall onto my knees and then we are face to face.

Now her eyes are wet. "Did a man hurt you?"

I nod.

"How?"

I look down and she says, "Look at me, how?" Her voice is calm but there is something very scary about the anger hidden inside it. The anger is not there for me but it's there. I start shivering even though it's not cold. "Who was it?" she asks, and then she says his name. "Was it him?" I start to shake even more. I start saying things. Heavy, thick, words fall out of me. They make water come out of my mami's eyes, but she's not making crying sounds. She's just looking at me. She wants me to say it all. When I'm finished, she brings me close to her. She holds me, she pets my hair. Now we are both crying. She tells me none of it was my fault. She promises that from now on, she will always protect me. She says she loves me more than anyone in the world. I ask her if she loves me more than Octavio and she laughs and says yes, more than Octavio. She leads me to my bed, she sings me a lullaby as if I were a baby, and we fall asleep together.

18

When I wake up, I hear my mami on the phone. She's standing in the kitchen next to the grumbling coffee machine trying to talk soft but I can hear every word she is saying. "I'm going to murder him," she says. "I'm going to go back there and kill him myself." She's trying to speak softly but she can't keep her voice down. She's quiet for a few moments, then she says, "Fine, then I will have him killed. I know people in San Marcos who can do that and I can afford it. I could have him dead by the end of next week. I'm going to tell them to make it slow."

I plug my ears. I don't like to think of my mami doing mean things. I fall asleep again. I dream of the curtain again but this time I can't see what's behind it. My mami's kicking something. I hear the man crying *stop, please stop!* When the curtains open, he's on the ground and he can't move.

My mami is sitting on my bed rubbing my back when I wake up. She says I don't have to go to school today. We are going to take a mini-vacation.

19

"I'll take you anywhere," she says. "Where do you want to go?"

I tell her to take me to my favorite spot in NYC, the Museum of Natural History. My mami likes the museum too. She likes to look at the still cats, their yellow eyes and golden fur. She smiles and hugs me. I forget about the things she said on the phone. I start to feel light and warm like the sunlight coming into the room.

On the train my mami asks me to tell her a story, which she almost never does. I get so excited I start talking loud and fast. "Shh, calm down," she says patting my legs. I try to speak quietly.

"Once upon a time, we were both mermaids. I was a blue mermaid and you were a bright, pink, beautiful mermaid. We had fish friends and they took us to Underwater Magic Land . . ."

My mami interrupts and steals the story from me, "On the way to the magic land you and I see a ferocious shark with fire eyes and a million teeth. He's hungry for us. I take out my sword and cut him in the face. He whimpers and swims straight down to the bottom of the sea where he will stay forever. Never to be seen again."

I laugh at my mami's shark and she laughs too. We keep telling stories like this back and forth all way to the museum. At the museum, we hold hands and talk about all the animals. Today I don't care if other eleven-year-olds don't hold their mami's hand. I feel for the first time ever that I am really hers and she is mine. I take her to the insects which I like best because you have to get really close to see their secrets. Today Mami likes the American deer and the foxes because they can live in the snow and winter and also in the sun. "They never lose their grace," she says. I could have stayed in the museum forever but my mami is carrying my baby brother inside of her so she gets tired. We get ice cream and sit on a bench in Central Park. The sun is just warm enough and the wind keeps coming and coming to wipe everything bad off of us.

20

I don't ever want to think of the chicken man again. I want to go into my brain and cut him out. I want to find him and snip him into little pieces, tiny, tiny, so that he will blow in the wind far away into the ocean and there the fish will eat him and he will turn into fish poop and then he will turn into . . . sand? I'm trying to think of a way to get rid of him completely. Lucia taps my shoulder as I'm walking up the stairs to first period.

"Where were you yesterday?" she asks.

"My mami and I went to the Natural History Museum."

Lucia raises her eyebrows. "You skipped school?"

I shrug and nod because Lucia can't know about the chicken man. All of a sudden I feel horrible like something you should step on and squish. Something gross not even a dirty stray dog would eat. I thought the sun and wind had cleaned me up but they didn't and I'm angry.

I don't want Lucia to ask me any more questions. At recess, I don't play jump rope with her and the nice girls. I run to Alice. We play her disgusting game of putting our fingers into our smelly mouths and then sticking them into boys' ears. The boys squeal like pigs and Alice and I cackle until we can't breathe.

21

Leah meets us in the lobby of her big building made out of glass and metal. She's wearing high heels and a pretty blue dress that matches her eyes. When I see her, I feel like being nice again. I tell her that when I grow up, I want to wear high heels and dresses and help girls like me. This makes her smile really big and she says, "That's the best thing I've heard all week." I feel proud and my mami puts her hand with freshly painted light pink nails on my shoulder.

We go to Leah's office. I wish I could bring sunshine and pretty drawings into her room with no windows but when she looks at me and my mami everything else disappears and I don't notice the empty dark walls. When she looks at us she makes us feel like nothing else matters and we are the only people in the world.

Leah says, "There's some good news." The translator says it in Spanish for my mami. She perks up the way she does when Octavio walks into the apartment. Leah explains that the government has given me a date for the interview.

Leah looks at me and says, "This is when an officer is going to ask you lots of specific questions about your life. He wants to know why you left El Salvador and why you should stay in the United States. You already know all the answers to the questions. He's asking about *your* life and no one knows more about your life than you."

I nod to show her that I agree but really, I feel a nasty feeling coming over. It's like a sewer smell, not there, but there, like something is very wrong and I can't say exactly what.

"And if you don't know the answer to one of his questions, you just say: I don't know. And that's completely fine. The point is to be honest. How does that sound?"

I look at my mami. Her hand goes around and around over my baby brother. She rubs her belly when she's nervous.

"And then they decide?" asks my mami.

"Then we wait two to three weeks."

"And then the decision is made?"

"Yes, but it's like we talked about on the phone. Elisa has a *really* strong case." Leah's eyes are sad and I know she knows. I know that my mami told her and it makes me feel a little better but also embarrassed. I know it's like my mami says, it wasn't my fault and I shouldn't feel bad or dirty, but I look down to the floor and feel my skin turn hot.

"But what if they say no?"

"We'll fight it. I will send in an appeal and we will get another chance and we will come back stronger."

My mami rubs her stomach.

"It's OK," I tell her, "I'm going to tell the truth and nothing but the truth so help me God." Leah and the translator laugh but my mami just bites her lip. She is in one of her dark moods.

My lawyer looks at me and says, "We are going to practice and I'm going to give you all the details so you are prepared. What do you think?"

I shrug because it's too hard to say what I think right now.

22

Leah tells me the officer will be in a tiny room. It will probably have no windows. He will sit in front of a computer and type every single word that I say. That makes me nervous. What if I say something silly and then it's in his computer forever? My lawyer tells me not to worry about that. She tells me to stick to what I know and that what I know is not silly. I like her answer but I don't know if I believe it. Then she tells us that the asylum building is not in NYC, it's in a small town called Bethpage. People from all over the world who have left their countries and want to stay in the United States are sent there to tell their stories to officers.

Leah says we are not going to be the only ones there and it will probably take hours for an officer to see us. She tells me she will bring markers and paper but that I should bring my favorite books and drawing things so that we don't get bored crazy. Then the translator tells my mami that she won't be able to come into the waiting room. It is dangerous for her. A group of people called ICE might come in and arrest her because she doesn't have a lawyer like I do. My mami tried to get a lawyer three times and each time the lawyers said no. They told her that her story was too complicated and too weak, which made my mami angry and sad. When I told her she should try again with another lawyer she shook her head and then said I shouldn't worry about her and her legal case, I should focus on mine.

Before we go to the asylum office in Bethpage, I practice the interview with Leah. She asks my mami to leave the room so that it feels real. She doesn't make me say the worst part but reads something she wrote about the chicken man in the right grown-up words. I wonder what the kids in my classroom would think if they heard it. I don't think they would believe it. *It's too horrible to be true,* someone would say. And I would reply: *HA! Got you. Just kidding!*

"What do you think?" she asks, her blue eyes are sadder than ever before. "Do you want me to add anything or take anything away?"

Everything feels mushy and slimy like a loose gray dream. My hands are sweaty and I wish I were anything besides a little girl. I think about my baby brother sleeping in my mami's belly and I am jealous of him. I want to start all over again. I don't want to have to wake up in my body. It hurts.

"Where were you born?" I ask Leah.

She tells me she was born and raised in a place called Boston and that her parents still live there.

I say, "What was your house like?"

She tells me it was quiet and peaceful and green. She used to climb a big tree in her front yard.

I ask her, "How many kids do you know like me?" I want to stop feeling like a freak.

She says, "Not a single one, Elisa. You are unique."

I say, "No, not like that. How many cases do you have?"

She gives a gentle smile. "Forty."

I know there are twenty kids in my classroom so I think of two classrooms filled with kids. Kids who might feel like me right now and that makes me feel less alone but also sad. I know it should maybe make me happy because it means all those kids have a nice lawyer but it doesn't. Leah and I sit in silence for a few moments.

"How do you feel about Monday?" she asks.

I say I feel ready. Then she takes me to the waiting room where my mami is sitting. On our way to the waiting room, I look at all the other lawyers in the office. For the first time I notice the folders on their desks. Folders and folders. They have names on them. Names of kids like me.

23

Before Monday, my mami has a baby shower. I think she does it so that we don't think about Monday. She is very nice about it and says that I can invite one of my friends. I think of inviting Alice but I decide to invite Lucia because she can speak Spanish. My mami says Lucia can come early and help decorate and I think Lucia will think that's fun.

My mami and I meet Lucia outside our building. Her papi drops her off in a nice black car and my mami whispers, "I didn't know your friend was rich." I shrug because I didn't know either. I didn't think about it until now and it makes me come up with a lot of questions about other kids at school and their nice clothes and backpacks and I realize a lot of them must be rich, much richer than me and my mami. All of a sudden I feel embarrassed and I wonder what Lucia will think of our small apartment because I don't have a room. I sleep on a little bed in the living room.

When we go up the elevator my hands start to get sweaty and I feel hot in the long-sleeve puffy dress my mami bought for me to wear to the party. It's white and blue to match all the decorations. Lucia smiles at me. She's wearing jeans, tennis shoes, and a t-shirt, and she has her pretty black hair down. I wish I looked like her, simple and clean. I think my dress is too tight and that Mami was right, I finally got fat from drinking all that juice and eating cookies and chips. But then Lucia says, "You look so pretty," and I start to feel a little better. When we walk into the apartment, she doesn't say anything about my bed being in the living room. She acts like it's normal. She talks in Spanish with Mami. Lucia asks her questions about my baby brother, like when he will be born and if he will go to the same school as us. My mami asks Lucia what her parents do for work. Lucia says doctor and banker and my mami nods and smiles. She seems happy that I have such a polite and pretty friend. She probably hopes that Lucia will rub off on me.

My mami asks Lucia if she has brothers and sisters and she says no.

"That's OK, you can come over anytime you want and help Elisa take care of her baby brother."

I like the idea of me and Lucia both being big sisters. I think of her coming over once my brother is born. Maybe by then I will already have my papers. My mami can teach us how to sing him lullabies in Spanish and everything will finally be OK.

We decorate the apartment with blue ribbons. Lucia knows how to make the ribbons look like roses and my mami is impressed. I know how to blow up balloons very big and very fast and my mami seems to like that too but not as much as Lucia's roses. When we are done the apartment looks completely different. Lucia takes a few steps towards the front door to take a good look. I do the same. We hung ribbons with roses off of every chair and the ceiling fan. We tied balloons together to look like flowers and stuck them onto the walls. My mami spread little bright pieces of silver paper on every table. Everything is shining. Even if we are poor, I don't think it looks like a poor person's apartment anymore.

"Wow! It's beautiful!" Lucia says right before Octavio walks in. He smiles really big when he sees what we have done, which I almost never see him do. He is carrying a big white box. He puts it down on the sparkly kitchen table and cuts the string off of it. It's a huge cake with blue and white frosting. In silver it says, *Welcome Bryan*. Lucia and I read it out loud at the same time.

"I don't like that name," I say.

My mami gives me a look. "It's a good name, very American."

"But why don't you give him a name from El Salvador? Isn't he from there too? Since you and Octavio are from there?"

She shakes her head. "Bryan will be American. You just wait and see."

Her words make me angry because I still want my baby brother to be from El Salvador. I make a promise to myself that I will tell him about the good things that happened to me in San Marcos. Like the time I made paper boats with Sarita and we sent them floating down the street after a storm. Or the times I played outside with my dogs and my friends. I could play as long as I wanted. We went into the campo with no grown-ups. Out in the fields the sun and the plants touched our skin. Those days made my heart feel wide open. When I think about them, I'm so happy I'm from El Salvador and I don't want anyone to tell me or my brother we're American.

Lucia can tell I'm a little sad. She says, "What's wrong?"

I tell her about Monday, how it's my asylum interview, and that I will have to tell an officer about all the awful things that happened to me in El Salvador.

"And then what?" she asks, her eyes are worried.

"Then my mami and I wait to see if the things were bad enough for them to let me stay."

"Were they really bad?"

I nod. I look down at my shoes, pink flats stepping on silver bits of paper.

Lucia takes off a necklace she is wearing. It's a beautiful sun made out of gold and it has diamond eyes. I think it must be very expensive.

"My tita in Mexico gave it to me," she says. "It's my good luck necklace. Every time we have a really hard test, I wear it and it works. I wasn't sure why I put it on today but now I know why . . . Wear it on Monday."

I want to believe in the necklace's powers but I also think that Lucia gets good grades on hard tests because she's smart. I don't say this. Instead, I hug her really tight and say thank you.

24

The morning of the interview my mami and I wake up very early to be at the train station. That's where we are going to meet Leah and the translator. Even though I don't really need a translator Leah says I should say everything in my first language. My mami tells me to wear a pink dress and she puts my hair into French braids. She tells me I need to look sweet and innocent. She wants the officer's heart to break when I walk through his door. Before we leave the apartment my mami makes me tuck Lucia's necklace under my dress. Suddenly she thinks it doesn't match. That annoys me but I'm too sleepy to argue.

The trains to Bethpage are not working so Leah orders us a car. It is my first time in a car since I moved to NYC. In the car, my mami is thinking about her journey to America. She tells the translator about it in Spanish. The car is rocking me to sleep so I only hear some of it: *It was too soon to bring Elisa, she was too little for it . . . on foot in the jungles, in the desert . . . my lips were as dry as paper . . . I thought I was going to die . . . Imagine her at four? No way . . . I don't know how those other women do it.*

My mami wakes me up. Now it's light out. We are outside the office in Bethpage in a big parking lot. There are no buildings around us, just a few trees, and a line of quiet, tired people. Leah gives me a banana and a granola bar. I tell her I'm really not hungry.

"Please try," says my mami. "You might not eat for hours." I take a few bites but only to make her happy. My stomach feels terrible and I want to curl up into a ball. Afterwards my mami fixes my hair and tidies up my dress. Finally, a guard opens the front door, the line of people starts to walk in. It's time to go. My mami and I give each other a big hug and I wave goodbye as I walk upstairs.

Upstairs guards walking around with guns on their belts look us up and down. "No food, no drinks, cellphones in lockers," they say over and over again. They look bored and grumpy. But I think I would be bored and grumpy too if I had to walk up and down a line saying the same thing over and over. I try to practice the interview questions in my head but I keep thinking about my mami. She's going to wait downstairs in another part of the building where there are no guards. She will probably be worried about me the entire time. I wish I could send her telepathic messages. I wish I could tell her I'm feeling brave.

After we put all of our bags and shoes into an x-ray machine like the ones at the airport in Texas, we go into the waiting room. It's a big and plain room with rows of chairs. It's painted the same yellowish color as all the folders I saw on the lawyers' desks. I look around the room. I see a white mommy with green eyes sitting with her baby, a black man in a fancy gray suit, a brown boy my age thumb-wrestling with his older brother, and more and more people who all want to stay in the United States, and I know they are not going to let us all stay.

Leah and my translator want to keep me busy. The translator says we should challenge each other to make crazy drawings. I tell her to make a chihuahua who likes to eat vegetables. She tells me to make a muddy pig who hates taking baths. My translator is really good at drawing and she says I'm talented. I challenge Leah to make a drawing of me. It comes out terrible and it makes the three of us laugh and laugh. The other people waiting smile. I ask Leah how long we have been in the room and she says three hours. That's when I realize I'm very hungry, but there's nothing we can do about it so I don't say anything. Finally, the serious woman in a dark blue suit who reads names off a list calls out, "Elisa López Diaz!" The sound of my name makes the three of us jump in our seats. We quickly put all the markers and papers away into my backpack.

We follow the woman in the suit down a hallway with no paintings, no pictures, no windows. It's so boring I want to fall sleep and scream at the same time. She takes us into an office where the officer sits in front of his computer. In his office there is also nothing on the walls and no windows. I imagined him big and mean but he's not. He has no hair on his head, he's skinny, he smiles. He reminds me of the rules Leah told me about: I can't get any help answering questions, Leah isn't allowed to talk until the very end, I need to answer everything slowly in Spanish, and, the most important rule, I can only tell the truth.

My translator says everything I say in Spanish in English. I listen to myself talk through her. It makes my life feel like it happened to her, instead of me. I keep answering question after question without even trying. The words just keep coming out. I tell the officer about my abuela hitting me, I tell him about sleeping on the floor, I tell him about going to school dirty and tired, and then not going to school at all, not because I didn't want to, but because my abuela wanted me to work instead. It's like I am asleep and in a dream, until he asks about the chicken man.

Then I wake up inside my body. I feel so tiny, like I could fit into a hand. I slide off the uncomfortable plastic chair and onto the carpet underneath the officer's desk. I don't want to look at anyone while I tell this part of the story. I still can't use the words Leah taught me. They are strong, real, grown-up words. Instead, I say thing, private thing, and pain. When I do I hold my knees to my chest very tight. I want to be a speck. I want to disappear forever. My translator and my lawyer touch my back and my hair. They help me sit back into the chair. In their eyes—one pair blue, the other black—I see they are proud of me and that they love me very much.

Finally, it's Leah's turn to talk. She's sitting behind me. I'm so tired that I can't hear her words. They float in and out of me, but still, I know what she means.

25

It will take two to three weeks for us to find out the government's decision. We don't talk about it, my mami and I, but I know we are both thinking about what will happen if I get sent back to El Salvador. Sometimes at night before I fall asleep, I think my mami would be happier without me. She could start fresh with Octavio and baby Bryan. I wouldn't be there to remind her how the world can be so mean. I think of the three of them at the Museum of Natural History looking at the insects, at the white foxes, and big cats, forgetting about me. Then I think about me in El Salvador back with my abuela. But this time I am different. Now I know that if someone hurts me, I will leave and never come back. I will escape and tell everyone I am an orphan. I will never mention my mami, my baby brother, Leah, school, Lucia, or NYC. I will make up a new story and a new name. I will turn into someone very different from Elisa. But deep down I don't want to be a new person. I'm starting to like who I am here. I fall asleep feeling so sad.

When the morning comes my mami wakes me up by kissing my forehead. I forgive her instantly for leaving me in El Salvador and for bringing me to America. I hug her belly where the baby sleeps. They smell like vanilla and honey. I say, "Mami, do you love me?" and she replies, as if it were the most obvious thing in the world, "Of course I do."

At school the days go by so slow and I really hate it. I start spending more recesses with Alice because if I didn't, I would eat all of Lucia's lunch just to do something different. Alice makes time go by a little faster. We start a game she invented where we try pinching the boys' butts. They hate it and they love it and they push us and give us bruises. Alice doesn't ask a lot of questions about my life like Lucia. She tells me about her crazy comic book ideas when we need to catch our breath. She says that when she grows up, she is going to become a famous director by turning her comic books into movies. Alice says that once she's famous she can help me sell my drawings. When I spend recess with Alice, I can tell Lucia gets a little sad. I want to tell her that I love her best but I keep forgetting to do it.

On better days that don't feel as slow, I can sit with Lucia at recess. I talk to her. I tell her that I am waiting for the decision and that my whole body feels zippy zappy. She says that I can keep the sun necklace until the government decides. She holds my hands and squeezes them really tight and tells me that she hopes with all of her heart that I can stay because she would miss me so much if I had to go back to El Salvador. I hope even more than Lucia hopes.

26

One day, I'm sitting on the couch playing with Kitty. My mami is cooking in the kitchen. It's a good day: it's raining, I didn't get in trouble at school, the house is full of good smells, I made a drawing of NYC, and my mami hung it on the fridge. Her cellphone rings. It's Leah. My mami's hands start to shake. She leans on the counter. I'm afraid she might faint so I stand next to her. She bursts into tears and starts laughing and crying and saying *gracias, gracias, gracias*, a hundred times *gracias*.

"You did it," she says, over and over. "You got asylum!"

She pulls me into her body and I can feel my baby brother kicking and squirming like he knows and is celebrating too. She fills my face with kisses and tears. I have never cried out of happiness before, and it feels good. I feel light afterwards, so many ugly worries have left my body. For the rest of the evening, I'm floating.

When Octavio walks in my mami yells out the good news and he gives me the biggest hug and I understand that he actually does love me. Maybe he understands that for the first time too. We all eat dinner and then Octavio takes us out for ice cream.

I don't go to school the next day. My mami and I go to Leah's office instead. She hugs us both for a long time. We sit down to look at the paper that says "Asylum granted." It's a small and thin piece of paper. I could tear it into little pieces if I wanted to. When I hold it in my hands, I think: the world is a weird place. I laugh and my mami and Leah laugh too because it seems like there is nothing left to do. My mami and Leah hug again and say goodbye. I don't think we will see her for a long time.

We get back on the subway. My mami has the little piece of paper in her purse and no one knows it. No one knows we are different now. I look at the other beautiful girls and wonder where they are going and where they came from. I make up stories for them and I wonder if they make up stories for me.

27

At school Lucia and I hug for a long time. She really squeezes me and it surprises me such a skinny girl can be so strong. I remind her about her gold sun necklace with the diamond eyes and she helps me take it off.

"See, I told you it was good luck," she says as I help her put it around her neck.

NYC is getting very cold now. We are outside at recess and we both have puffy coats on and Lucia's nose is a pretty red button. I never thought a place could get so cold and gray. On the grayest days, I miss El Salvador and the campo and the animals so much it makes my heart feel like it's thumping deeper in my chest. Leah said I can't go back to El Salvador, at least not for a very long time. My mami said, "Good! Why would you want to go back? To what?"

I look at the little sun shining on Lucia's chest. We are silent for a bit.

"I'm going to Mexico," she says, "For Christmas, to visit my tita."

I get jealous immediately, but I don't show it. Instead, I say, "That's cool."

But Lucia doesn't seem happy. I almost feel like running away from her for being so ungrateful. I look over at Alice who is playing basketball with three boys. She falls on her butt and yells out some bad words. I smile. I'm about to tell Lucia I'm going to play with them and that I'll catch up with her later but she holds my hand.

"My tita is very sick," she says. "Mami says it might be the last time we see her."

Her eyes fill up with tears. I've never seen my friend so sad. I feel guilty for wanting to get rid of her. I want to be good for her like she was for me. We walk around the playground like that in silence holding hands because I think that's what I would want if someone I loved was going to die. Sometimes there's nothing to say.

"When are you leaving?" I ask when the bell rings.

"On Saturday."

"I'm going to miss you," I say and I really mean it.

Lucia

Dear Tita,

I'm writing to you on the plane. Mami and I are on our way back to the city. You died a week ago and I don't understand it . . . I won't be able to talk to you on the phone, or send you emails with my questions, and when I go to Mexico in the summer you won't be there. Mami says it's OK to be confused and that there is nothing wrong with the way I'm feeling. Sad and jumbled up.

People cried and cried at your funeral. Young people, old people, students, professors, cleaning ladies, janitors, cousins, aunts, uncles, and me too. I cried. Mami cried. I think she will miss you the most because Tito died a long time ago before I was born. I don't think Papi cried but I'm not sure since he wasn't at your funeral. He had to leave Mexico early because now he is vice president at the bank and has many more responsibilities. I could tell Mami was sad but she didn't say anything about it. Mami never complains. She is always so calm. You said that I'm a lot like her . . . *so serene, so pretty, so wise.* When Papi left Mexico early, I didn't complain either.

Mami is closing her eyes right now. I think she hasn't really slept since you died. Maybe she's dreaming about you and talking to you like I'm talking to you right now in my head. When I asked her where she thinks you went after you died, she just shrugged and gave me a little smile. Maybe heaven does exist and maybe you are in it. I can see you in a garden with bougainvillea, cacti, a papaya tree . . . a rabbit, a dog, and a parrot. You take care of the dead pets of people who are still alive until it's their turn to go to heaven. I see you stretching out your old creaky bones to fly. These are nice thoughts but if I'm really being honest, I have no idea at all of where you are and I don't think anyone else really knows either.

Te quiero,
Lucia

Dear Tita,

I went back to school today. Everyone had already been back from winter break for days and they were used to everything again. Not me. I wanted to be back in Mexico on your rooftop with you and Mami and the big dog Rulfo drinking agua de jamaica. I didn't want to be in cold New York and I didn't want to see anyone at all. Expect for Elisa. She ran up to me before first period and hugged me so tight I coughed a little. She asked me about you right away, "Se murió?" I nodded and held back my tears. Elisa hugged me again and could feel Lola and Julio and Alice watching us and I started to get embarrassed. I was happy when Mr. G shouted, "Hey! Listen up!"

During class Elisa and I wrote each other notes back and forth. Elisa had lots of questions about you and Mexico. She wanted to know if you had a job and what kind of house you lived in and if you had any maids. I told her you taught medicine at the University, that you lived in a big beautiful house with lots of plants and colors, and that yes, you had a maid. The questions made me feel weird because Elisa's family in El Salvador is poor and I don't think she would go to a big, nice, clean house if she ever went back.

It was a gray day and I felt just like it. I did my homework fast and sloppy which you know I never do. Then I curled up on the couch and tried to read a new book from the library about a girl who is living through the end of the world but my mind kept pulling me out of it. I'm not used to being this sad and I'm not sure what you are supposed to do with it. Wait? I looked out the window until Mami came home and then we both had chamomile tea with honey and talked about you. That made it a little better.

Te quiero,
Lucia

Dear Tita,

I have to tell you something. Yesterday I went into Mami and Papi's room because I wanted to ask Mami a science question. But I couldn't ask her the question because she was taking a shower. You know how she likes to take showers after work, before dinner, to clean the hospital off of her. Underneath the sound of the water, I could hear her crying.

The only time I ever saw her crying was when you died. But when she cried about you, she didn't make a sound. At your velorio quiet water just rolled out of her eyes. But this time when I pressed my ear to the door of the bathroom, I could hear that her tears were angry. I could have asked but I didn't. She might have been embarrassed and I didn't want to make things worse.

The weirdest part was that at dinner Mami tried to act all normal. Her eyes were a little puffy but Papi didn't notice. He talked about the bank. It's going very well. He had a big smile on his face. I know the smile means more money. We have a lot of money, Tita. It comes and comes. Mami smiled back at him, but just a little smile.

Mami told me that when you just met my Papi you said, *el que quiere arañar la luna, se arañará el corazón*. It is something a poet said a long time ago. It means that people who want to claw at the moon will end up scratching up their own hearts . . . right? I always thought it was mean you said it and I never understood why you did, but something about the way Papi talked about the bank during dinner made me remember it.

Now in my mind I see Papi jumping and jumping towards the beautiful, shiny, white moon, getting so tired, and never being able to reach it.

I feel like something's wrong, Tita. What is it?

Te quiero,
Lucia

Dear Tita,

I didn't feel so great this morning. I woke up with a headache. I told Mami, but she said what I knew she was going to say: *it will go away.* She rubbed a minty balm on my forehead which she said you always did for her and after first period I noticed the headache was gone. Mami is usually right about things.

During recess I asked Elisa, "Is your mami usually right about things?"

She thought about it for second and then said, "She sometimes hits my hand or twists my ear really tight. I know I could get her into a lot of trouble if I told a teacher about it . . . In America that type of thing is bad."

"Are you going to tell a teacher?" I asked.

"Of course not!" Elisa said rolling her eyes at me. "Most of the time I deserve it. I can be a very bad."

I asked her if she could be as bad as Alice who really seems like a spoiled brat to me. Elisa laughed, "I can be a lot worse." Part of me didn't believe Elisa at all, but another part got a little scared and wondered if I should keep trying to make her my best friend.

The rest of recess we played tag. Alice ran the fastest and was the hardest one to catch. Sometimes instead of just touching someone she would push them. I thought about telling her to stop but I wasn't feeling brave. After recess I felt like telling Elisa about hearing Mami cry in the shower, but when I looked around to find her, she was whispering things into Alice's ear and that made not want to tell her anything at all.

The next class was English Language Arts and even though it's my favorite class I felt tired. I stared out the window at the cloudless sky and thought about Mexico and how it was 11 AM there. I imagined the sun shining on your rooftop garden. The chiles, the passionfruit, and the cacti are growing without you.

Te extraño,
Lucia

Dear Tita,

It is Wednesday. I came home from school and I sat down to do my homework on the kitchen table. I ate a snack: mango with lime and chili. I thought of you and your crooked hands cutting fruit. Mami wanted to cut the fruit for you but you just swatted her away. You said your crooked hands still worked fine and I liked that you said that. Did you always say what was on your mind? Or did you only start doing that when you became an old lady?

I thought I was alone in the apartment but all of a sudden Papi came out of the bedroom. He wasn't in a suit like he usually is when he comes home from work. He was in weekend clothes, dark blue jeans, a white shirt, clean sneakers. Mami tells me Papi is very handsome and I never understood what she meant until today.

We were both surprised to see each other.

"What are you doing here?" he said. "Don't you have writing club?"

He seemed angry at me and I didn't understand because I didn't do anything wrong. I told him writing club was on Thursday. Then I asked him why he was at home. He said he had decided to leave work early because he had errands to run. I asked him if I could go with him.

He looked sad and touched my hair in a nice way. Soft and gentle. "No, corazón," he said. "Stay here and do your homework."

When he left, the apartment felt very lonely and empty, even though it didn't feel like that when I thought I was by myself. I went to Papi's office and sat in his big comfy chair. I typed "Coyoacán" into his computer to see pictures of your neighborhood. I cried for a little looking at the famous fountain with the two coyotes, one calm, the other one growling. We used to make up different stories about why one of them was so angry. Some days he was right but other days he was just exaggerating. "He's a little moody," you would whisper into my ear so that the coyote wouldn't hear.

A message appeared on the side of Papi's screen. I wiped my tears away with my sweater. A new email. Without thinking I clicked on it.

It said: Are you coming tomorrow? ♥ Anna

I sat still because the world froze. *Who the heck is Anna?* I thought. *Why is she sending Papi a heart?* I was about to type in "Anna" in the search bar of Papi's email but I heard Mami's keys in the door. I turned the screen off.

"Hola bonita!" she shouted from the hallway. My throat felt so dry I didn't know if I could respond. "Hi Mami," I croaked back. She entered the office. She was wearing her fitted black scrubs and the fleece jacket with her name stitched over her heart, Dr. Bracamontes. I was about to tell her everything but she was smiling big and she started to tell me about a liver transplant she had done that day. "A Mexican grandmother," she said, still smiling. "We thought we weren't going to get the organ, but it came through and she's alive." I hadn't seen her smile so much since you died and I didn't want to ruin it.

"I'll tell you more about it after my shower," she said, letting her long black wavy hair out of a tight ponytail. It spilled onto her shoulders and down her back. "It was kind of magical."

I could hear Mami singing under the water. One of those old songs in Spanish that you taught her. I turned back Papi's monitor and went back to the email and marked it as unread so that he would never know that I had seen it. I felt like a liar. I don't like to keep secrets, especially from Mami and Papi.

Te quiero mucho,
Lucia

Dear Tita,

Papi said we should go to the movies on Saturday. Just the two of us. Papi almost never has time to do this. You know how hard he works. All the time. I felt weird about going out with him alone. I was scared that he knew I knew something I wasn't supposed to know. I must have looked awkward because he said, "What, you don't want to do something?" He seemed a little sad and that made me feel horrible.

"No! I do . . . it's just . . . can I invite Elisa?"

Papi knows Elisa lives far away, all the way up in the Bronx.

"Can we pick her up in the car?" I asked.

Papi looked at Mami and made a face. Mami gave him a look like he shouldn't complain. She likes that I'm friends with

Elisa, who is different from the Upper West Side girls and speaks perfect Spanish.

Papi rolled his eyes but said, "OK, princesa. We can pick her up in the car."

I made a little dance because I love taking the car with Papi. We listen to Vicente Fernández and Chavela Vargas and sing the words together like we were really tough or really heartbroken. Papi and Mami smiled. They almost never see me do things like that because I'm what people call an introvert. I almost forgot about the email from Anna but then I remembered and it made me sit down all of a sudden. Papi thought it was a joke and he laughed. Mami gave me a confused look. "Are you OK, amor?"

I made sure to give them a nice smile so that he wouldn't think anything was wrong.

Te extraño,
Lucia

Dear Tita,

I had a strange dream last night. You were teaching me how to cut Papi's hair in the patio under the guava tree next to the pool. I think it had just stormed because there were guavas all over the floor. They were like little pink smashed brains except they smelled sweet. And in walked Mami with her hair down, not in a ponytail like she always has it when she is Dr. Bracamontes. It was down to her hips like an Aztec princess. She said, *I want a haircut too.* You put her beautiful long hair in a braid and cut the braid off.

Then, the real Mami woke me to go to school. I told her about the dream and that's when she said maybe you were trying to tell me something.

"What is she trying to say?" I asked.

She shrugged. "I don't know. Maybe we aren't ready to understand yet."

I didn't like Mami's answer. I thought and thought about it at school. I thought about Rapunzel and how she let her long gold hair down a tower so a knight could climb it and help her escape. I drew her in her tower alone with short hair. Her long blond braid was in a pile on the grass. Now she would have to think of an escape plan all on her own. I felt Alice looking over my shoulder.

"Nice," she said. Even though I don't like Alice, that compliment still felt good because Alice is the best at drawing. But I still didn't want her asking any rude questions about my drawing, so I covered it with my hands.

"Alice, please sit down!" Ms. Lee shouted.

Everyone giggled and Alice stomped back to her chair. Her combat boots made an extra loud noise. I had a thought that maybe part of me did like Alice for always doing what she wants and always saying what she thinks. I wondered what Alice would've done if she had seen messages from Anna on her dad's computer. I think she would have started yelling about it right away. She would've stomped all over her house. She might have even broken some plates like they do when they are mad in the movies. What am I doing about it? Nothing. Just writing. I don't know if that's the right thing. I don't know anything at all.

Te extraño,
Lucia

Dear Tita,

Today, Papi, Elisa, and I went to the movies.

On the way to the Bronx, Papi put on his music, our music, loud. We sang and sang all the way to Elisa's apartment. I forgot about Anna. I even forgot about missing you. We parked outside of Building B of the Rosewood Parkway Houses. Rosewood Parkway makes the place sound nice, but it's not very nice. Papi said Elisa's type of building is called "the projects" and that's where the city puts poor people.

"What do you mean puts poor people?" I asked.

"Everything else in New York is too expensive so people who can't afford the rents that are normal, but shouldn't be normal, live there."

"How much do we pay for rent?" I asked while I looked up at the windows. They're a lot smaller than ours and the had black metal bars on them which made them seem like cages and made the whole building seem like a place you could get trapped in it forever.

"I don't think you want to know." Papi looked at his watch and sighed. "Your friend is late."

"More than three thousand dollars?"

Papi laughed. "How about more than three times that?"

I didn't know what to say, Tita. For some reason I felt embarrassed.

Finally, Elisa appeared with her pretty mami. She saw me standing next to Papi. His arm around my shoulder, both us leaning on the BMW. Her eyebrows went up her forehead and I felt myself blush. I wished that Papi had a more normal car. But Papi is good at meeting new people. He's good at smiling and coming up with words, which made everything less awkward. He was very nice to Elisa's mami. She was wearing a tight black dress underneath her coat that showed her perfectly round belly with a baby growing inside of it. A long braid went down her back. The gold necklaces and earrings she wore shone in the winter sun. I wondered if Papi thought she was as beautiful as I thought she was. Elisa touched her mami's belly. Her hand went around and around in a circle and I wanted to do the same while Elisa's mami and Papi spoke in Spanish, but I'm a little scared of Elisa's mami. I know she can be strict sometimes. I know she can turn from nice to mean all of a sudden with no explanation. Elisa said it's always better to stay on her good side. I tried hard to smile extra sweet at her.

In the car, Elisa was so excited she kept taking her seatbelt off to look out of one window and the next. She bumped into me over and over. If I did that Papi would have gotten mad and told me to put my seatbelt on right away. Instead, he laughed at the crazy things Elisa said and turned the music up so that the ride felt like a party. For a second, I thought maybe I had chosen the wrong best friend and that maybe Alice and Elisa should've gone to the movies without me. Just as I was thinking that Elisa stuck her head out of the window and let her two ponytails flap in the cold wind. She started to howl like wolf and I couldn't help but laugh and then I liked Elisa all over again.

Once we were in the dark cool movie theatre, Elisa got quiet and calm and I think I did like it better that way. I sat in between her and Papi. Before the movie started Elisa whispered into my ear, "I have never been to a movie theatre before."

I looked at her. "Really? Aren't there movies in El Salvador?"

"Yeah," she said. "Just no one ever took me."

I didn't know if I should feel happy or sad for Elisa so I just took her hand and squeezed it. In the movie there was a lady superhero with long blond ponytails, shorts, fishnet tights, and boots. She seemed like one of those comic characters Alice likes to draw in her notebook, and Elisa loved her. I liked watching her big eyes get sparkly in the dark. Then I turned to see Papi's reaction and I saw him looking at his phone. I thought of Anna again. Was Papi texting her? Was she sending him more hearts? My mouth went so dry. I have never felt thirstier in my life. I took huge gulps of Elisa's enormous Coke.

At the end of the movie Papi told us he had to make a business call and that we should wait for him by the water fountain. I wanted to say something about Papi aloud. I could feel the words thumping inside my mouth. Elisa talked and talked about the movie and I couldn't hear anything.

I blurted, "I think my papi was sending messages to a woman during the movie . . . A woman who isn't my mami."

Elisa got a strange little smile on her face. She covered her mouth.

"What?" I said. "Say it." I grabbed her hands and tried to take her fingers off her mouth one by one. Elisa shook her head. She giggled and giggled. I squeezed her cheeks like if I could squeeze words out of her and watch them all fall onto the floor. "Ouch!" Elisa cried, still laughing, and holding her cheeks which I'd left red marks on.

"I'm sorry," I said. "But, I really want you to just say it."

"He's probably cheating . . ." Elisa said. "Behind your mami's back."

My face got hot. I plugged my ears to not hear any more.

Elisa tried unplugging my ears. I tried getting away from her and then making my arms stiff, but she's stronger than me. "You know I'm right," she said, a little out of breath.

I wanted to slap Elisa across the face. I wanted her skin to sting the way my throat stung. But Papi came out of the bathroom and gave us both a big smile. Elisa smiled back. I think I must have looked sick because Papi touched my shoulder and asked, "Too much candy?"

I nodded.

In the car I was very quiet. Elisa kept looking at me with big curious eyes and a little guilty smile. I think she felt bad that she was being silly about the whole thing and realized that it was actually a big deal to me. She put her head on my shoulder and at first, I wanted to nudge her off but for some reason I didn't. I leaned my head on top of hers.

Te quiero mucho,
Lucia

Dear Tita,

I'm writing to you on a Sunday night. You taught us that Sundays are días de familia, when family needs to spend the whole day together. Usually, I like Sundays. They have a warm cozy feeling to them. But not this Sunday. I felt like Papi and I were lying to Mami and that I was lying to both of them and that Papi was lying to us. Could she feel any of the lies underneath everything? Like when you feel a little rumble underneath the cement and it's a gigantic subway rushing past you underground? It felt evil to trick such a good person like Mami.

We were sitting at Leonidas, one of our regular spots. In the same place as always in a booth near the window. It was rainy and cold out. Usually, the red leather chairs and the pretty glass lamps giving off a warm glow cheer me up, but not today. I looked out the window with my head in my hands.

"Why so quiet?" Papi said taking a hold of my braid from across the table. It made my skin prickle. I shrugged and looked out the window again. I felt Papi give Mami a look. Mami just shrugged. That's when I saw Alice and her parents making their way into the restaurant.

"Ugh . . ."

"What is it?" asked Mami.

"Alice is coming in . . . she's so annoying."

"The girl from your class?" said Papi. "The one who always gets in trouble?"

Mami pressed her finger to her mouth.

Alice's short blond hair was even messier than how she wore it at school. She had painted a patch of it blue. She was wearing all black, her pair of silver combat boots, and a leather jacket that was too big on her. I actually kind of liked how she looked. She pointed at me and the three of them walked towards our table.

"Dr. Bracamontes! How nice," said Alice's mom. "Hello Lucia."

I smiled back at her. She was the opposite of Alice with her long brown hair, happy green eyes, and a colorful scarf dangling to all the way to her knees. Alice told Elisa once that she used to be famous singer. She also told Elisa that her dad was still a famous jazz musician. He was standing next to her mom. He had small round sunglasses on and was a lot shorter that his wife. I wondered if his tousled gray hair used to be blond like Alice's. Probably. As our parents made small talk Alice gave me an unexpected sweet smile which I thought was strange. I had only ever seen her be nice to Elisa. Maybe once or twice to Lobo when they weren't making fun of each other.

"What an *interesting* family," Papi said when they left to their table.

"I think they're nice," said Mami. "They're just . . . eccentric."

"You think they could tell their daughter to comb her hair a little and wear some decent clothes."

Mami's eyes narrowed. "Please don't criticize an eleven-year-old in front of Lucia. It's not a good example."

A pretty waitress interrupted their argument. I saw how Papi forgot about Alice and her parents right away. He talked to her with his eyes and his mouth saying things to her that weren't the words he said. I saw his secrets hanging off of him like something shiny I could touch. I saw the waitress smile back at him with a special smile that I think she saves for nice-looking men like Papi. I looked over at Mami and she was looking down at her phone. She didn't notice a thing or maybe she was pretending not to notice. When the waitress asked what I wanted, I didn't know. I searched through the menu.

Papi said, "She will have the Pasta Bolognese."

I felt my skin prickle again. Little needles were landing on top of my head, on my shoulders, and arms. I looked over at Alice. She was sitting with her knees to her chest. Both of her feet on the chair. She was reading a book. She didn't care about getting dirty or about what other people thought. Not one bit.

Without thinking, I said, "I'll choose for myself, thank you very much."

The waitress raised her eyebrows, Papi let out a little chuckle, and Mami looked up from her phone. I picked the ravioli and the waitress walked away.

"Mi amor, don't talk to your Papi in that tone. It's not nice," my mami said and I could tell she was disappointed in me.

I wanted to cry but that would've been very weird so I stood up and went to the bathroom and cried a little in the stall, very quietly, hoping that Alice wouldn't come barging in to ask me any questions.

Te extraño,
Lucia

Dear Tita,

Today during recess, I remembered you with Elisa and I told her that I miss you and that I wish we could talk. Then Elisa told me about her abuela. She said it like a story. "Once upon a time there was a mean old witch that made a little girl do horrible chores all day every day—wake up early in the morning to work before school, mop and sweep every day all by herself, wash all the dishes, clean the clothes by hand, cook over a hot stove, clean all the animal poop . . . And if the girl didn't do these things, the witch would hit her back with a telephone cord, or make her sleep in the closet on a dirty old towel, or . . . worse! Much worse!"

I didn't know what to say. Part of me thought Elisa lied or maybe part of me wished it all really was just a sad made-up story. Another part knew it was the truth. Elisa laughed her wild, loud laugh. Then she munched on her chips. Little bits flew out of her mouth. Sometimes she makes me feel squirmy. I looked around the cafeteria. Alice was sitting by herself, drawing, and she looked up to watch Elisa cackle. No one else paid attention.

Elisa drew me in close and whispered into my ear, "I know how to talk to the dead. I can help you with your abuelita." Her breath was warm and smelled sour. I had the feeling I feel a lot when I am around Elisa, wanting to get away from her, and at the same time wanting to stay very close.

"You know, my abuelita was a mean old witch but she wasn't stupid. It's because of her that I know how to do a lot of things. Like run a fruit stand and kill a chicken and train dogs and talk to spirits. All we need is a dark room, a candle, a mirror, and something that used to be your Tita's."

Even though I know ghosts aren't real, I started getting nervous.

"And you probably also need me because I have experience," Elisa added. "C'mon, invite me to sleep over and we can try it! It will be fun."

Today I'm asking Mami if I can invite Elisa to sleep over. Part of me thinks Elisa has no idea how to talk to spirits. She lies a lot. I caught her yesterday. We were walking back to class after recess and out of the blue for no good reason she told Lola, the most popular girl, that she used to be a model in El

Salvador. Elisa said it so seriously that Lola believed her. I sent her a note in class that said, *Was the model thing true?* Elisa covered her mouth as she giggled so Ms. Luz wouldn't scold her. She wrote back: *What do you think?*

The point is I don't know if Elisa knows anything about darkness, mirrors, spirits, but I will try anyway. I'd like to ask you what I should do about Papi and Anna and Mami. I'd like for you to tell me if I should just lock it up in my brain and keep it.

Te quiero mucho,
Lucia

Dear Tita,

Elisa is coming over on Saturday. We made a secret plan during recess: I'm going to take a mirror from Mami and Papi's bathroom. Sometimes Mami uses it to put on lipstick but she almost never wears lipstick these days. Elisa is going to bring a candle with a santo on it. She says her mami has at least twenty of them (which probably means she has ten) and that she won't miss it. Then, I will take matches from a drawer in the kitchen where Papi puts his collection of match boxes he takes from fancy restaurants. Finally, I will take a doll you gave me for my eighth birthday. I used to love her with all of my heart. She is made out of fabric and she smells like sun and dirt. She has black thread eyes and a pink dress. I picked her out of hundreds all the same except a little different because they were all made by hand. Do you remember? I will sit her against the candle to talk to you. Elisa said that the trick is to turn off all of the lights, except the candle, and to point the mirror in a way where you can only see darkness in it. When they are ready the spirits will show up, not in the room, but inside of the mirror.

Does all of this seem silly?

Te quiero,
Lucia

Dear Tita,

Last night I started to get nervous. It all felt sort of stupid and embarrassing. Maybe deep down I was actually scared. I wanted Elisa to forget about the whole plan. I told myself, *Don't say anything about it, distract her.* I told her we should make cupcakes, so we did. I told her we should make up a dance and record ourselves, so we did. I told her we should watch a movie, and we did. I wanted Elisa to get sleepy and forget it. But she didn't.

It was dark outside. Mami still wasn't home. She was having a late night at the hospital. Papi was busy in his office, still working with the door closed. He wasn't paying any attention to us. Elisa's eyes, even though they are black, remind me of the moon sometimes. They got so enormous, full of light. "It's time now," she said, "to talk to your abuelita."

She asked me for the mirror, the matches, and the doll. Because I knew she would get super mad if I didn't get them, I obeyed. When she lit the candle, she told me to turn off the light.

"Sit here," she said pointing to a spot on my carpet. "Here you will be able to see the mirror, but not your face in the mirror."

I obeyed and sat but Elisa scowled.

"No, no, no, no . . ." She pushed me just an inch. "Now, *that's* the perfect place." She gave me a very serious look and said, "Now you have to concentrate really hard on this or it won't work. You have to think about your abuelita and her espíritu."

I wanted to ask Elisa what she meant but she kept going.

"Close your eyes and think," Elisa commanded.

I thought about you, Tita, and my heart started to thump. I thought about you feeding the stray black cat in the patio, how you told me you didn't give it a name because the cat didn't want one. I thought of you sitting by the pool reading a book. I liked to bring you limonada and you liked it when I put my head in your warm lap.

Elisa broke the silence, she said, "Son bienvenidos." She said it many times and told me to say it with her. *You are welcome here, you are welcome here, you are welcome here.* She said that the spirits needed to feel safe to come into the mirror to talk to us. I wondered what spirit Elisa was thinking about. Her voice was strong and it sounded much older than an eleven-year-old's. It was scaring me. Her breath was becoming like a strong wind. Wind that could blow something over. Would she blow the candle onto my carpet? Would she burn up the whole room? I was going to say, *Elisa, please stop.* But it was too late. She let out a long and horrible scream that made my whole body stiff.

"I saw him! I saw him," she said. "It means he's dead! It means my mami got him killed!"

I had no idea what Elisa was talking about and I didn't even have time to think about it because Papi burst into the room.

"What is happening here?" He looked around the room

with worried eyes. He looked for danger, but only saw the mirror, the candle, and the doll, and his face relaxed.

"What are you girls up to?"

"Nothing . . ." I said. "We're just . . . playing."

"Come into my office, Lucia."

"No!" Elisa said. "You can't leave me alone!"

I looked at her to see if she was acting, but it didn't seem like it. She actually looked scared and Papi saw it too. He sighed a deep sigh and sat on my carpet.

"That didn't sound like 'just playing.' You know, you're a bad liar, Lucia." Papi pet my hair. The word liar coming out of his mouth made my face hot.

"You're a bad liar too," I replied, looking at him straight in the eyes. Papi squirmed. For a second, I wondered if Elisa's magic had worked and if you were actually in the room. Maybe it was you speaking through me. For a moment, Papi knew exactly what lies I was talking about and he didn't like it one bit. Elisa knew too. The three of us sat in silence.

Papi cleared his throat. "All I can say is that you shouldn't be playing these scary games. It's not for good girls like you two."

My eyes filled with tears and I bit my tongue to hold them inside of me.

"I'm not a good girl," said Elisa.

Papi laughed. "Yes you are, corazón. Now let's go to the kitchen and make something nice. A hot chocolate?" Elisa nodded wiping the tears and snot off her nose with the end of her long-sleeve shirt. I followed them into the kitchen.

After the hot chocolate Elisa was acting like nothing had ever happened, like her scream hadn't paralyzed me and Papi, like she hadn't begged us not to leave her alone.

"Who did you see?" I asked her. "Who's dead?"

Elisa's eyes narrowed and then she let out an exaggerated yawn.

"I'm soooooo tired," she said and she fell asleep right away. I'm up writing to you before I turn off the light.

Buenas noches,
Lucia

Dear Tita,

This morning it was just me and Mami and Elisa. Where was Papi? I didn't ask. Mami made us pancakes with blueberries in them. She said that when she was a little girl in Mexico she never had pancakes. She said you usually made her molletes with butter and sugar and a licuado de chocomilk con banana. She said she loved it. I like it when Mami talks about you and Mexico. She said that on weekend mornings she didn't hear the sounds of the city coming up into her windows floating up from the street like I do now. She didn't hear the footsteps of the neighbors on the seventh floor or their little dog running down the hall. In the morning she heard doves and sparrows in trees, the dogs barking from rooftops, an old man sweeping fallen leaves with his broom, the calls of a fruit vendor.

Mami looked at me and said, "We are having such different childhoods." I didn't know if she sounded a little sad.

I asked, "Which one is better?"

Mami smiled and said, "Neither, mi amor. Things aren't always black and white, better or worse, you know that."

We were all quiet for a bit and then Mami said, "Do you want to talk about last night?"

Elisa looked up from her pancakes, licked the maple syrup off her lip, and said, "No, thank you!"

Mami chuckled and then we all laughed. For a second, I got filled up with a warm feeling like if everything was OK.

Te quiero,
Lucia

Dear Tita,

Something interesting happened at school today. Alice came into Ms. Luz's class looking so sad and angry. Her big red combat boots made a loud sound and everyone turned to look. Then Alice put her head on the desk and started to cry! I won't even let myself cry in front of Mami but Alice didn't seem to care about crying in front of the whole classroom. That's when Lola, the meanest and the prettiest girl in the whole grade whispered, "Weirdo." Alice turned around and said, "Shut the f— up you b—." Elisa cackled.

I have a feeling you were more like Alice than like me when you were a little girl. Mami said you always spoke what was on your mind. Sometimes I wish I didn't plan things in my mind before doing them and instead I just did them right away without being afraid.

Ms. Luz sent Alice to the office. A few minutes later Elisa said she had to go to the bathroom but I think she was pretending. I bet she went to go look for Alice, just to see what they were going to do to her. Elisa might not always say what's on her mind, but she usually does what she feels like doing. I can't, Tita. I like doing the *right* thing. The thing Mami and Papi would want me to do. That's why this is all so hard. I don't know what Mami and Papi would want me to do and I can't ask them.

Te quiero,
Lucia

Dear Tita,

I decided I wanted to talk to you again this time without Elisa. Mami and Papi were still at work. I turned off all the lights and I lit the candles Elisa left under my bed. I had Mami's mirror and my muñeca set up just like Elisa had showed me. I said, *Tita no tengo miedo, Tita ven a visitarme, Tita please come tell me what to do.*

At first there was nothing. I was staring into the mirror and I didn't see anything but darkness and I started to get sleepy. A funny thing happened when I closed my eyes and laid on the carpet. I heard a voice in my head and the voice wasn't your voice as I expected, it was my voice. It said: *Tita is not gone. She is in your blood and in your bones.* The voice was clear and I understood what Elisa meant by espíritu. Your spirit is swimming in the veins of my arms up into my brain, through my heart, down my stomach and legs. And now, I'm thinking that if part of you is in me, a part of me must have been in you. You took it with you when you went back into the earth. All those memories you have of me when I just came out of Mami's stomach, when I was wrapped up in a white blanket like a cocoon, they were turned into ashes, and now they are feeding the soil of a tree where a hummingbird builds her little nest.

A beautiful feeling came over me that made me feel like even though things end they turn into something else. I felt for the first time in a long time that I didn't have to worry about whatever happened next because nothing could ever stay the same anyway.

I heard Mami's keys in the door. I opened my eyes, blew out the candles, and hid them under my bed.

Te quiero,
Lucia

Dear Tita,

I told Elisa about your espíritu in me, about my espíritu in you, about things not dying forever, just changing into something else. She looked at me in a strange way like if she was trying to see if I was lying. Maybe that's the look I give her a little bit too much. When she decided I was telling her the truth she said, "What are you going to do about it?"

"Do about what?"

"Dead people don't give messages out for nothing. You are supposed to do something about the things they tell you."

I don't know where Elisa gets her rules. Maybe from her mami or her mean abuela. Or maybe she just makes them up while she's talking.

"What did you do with your message?"

Elisa gave me a dirty look. "My message was different. The espíritus told me about something that has already been solved and it's none of your business."

I wanted to argue with her, but instead I started crying. It was like if all the tears I'd been holding since I found out about Papi and Anna burst out of me. I was embarrassed. I hid in Elisa's shoulder and wet her long black hair. Elisa didn't seem surprised or annoyed.

Te quiero mucho,
Lucia

Dear Tita,

I think it was you who woke me up this morning. I never wake up before the sun on the weekend. The apartment was still dark, just thin lines of sunlight through the curtains. I woke up and I was wide awake. I felt ready. *Ready for what?* I asked my brain. And it said: *Ready for being brave.* I walked out into the kitchen and there was Papi in his work clothes but it didn't look like he was going to the office. His hair wasn't wet and neat. His eyes were red. All the bravery I had just a second before abandoned me, but I didn't run back to my room or pretend I was just grabbing a glass of water. I stood still and looked at him.

"Hola Lucy," he said and he smiled.

"Hola Papi," I said, "I need to say something to you."

He put his coffee cup down. I still had time, I thought, to keep it in, to lie, to help him keep lying. I took a deep breath and then said, "I know about Anna. I know you're cheating on Mami."

My words hit Papi in the heart like the sharpest arrow. We looked at each other. *Was Papi going to lie it all away?* I wondered. I think he was debating it. But he looked so tired. All he could do was put his head in his hands. I didn't like to see Papi so sad. *Was he crying?* I wondered. *What would I do if he was crying?* I stood there frozen. Papi did finally look at me and then he put hands out for me to hold them. I wasn't angry at him at all even though maybe I should've been angry. I was just sad for making him sad and sad that he made us all sad. I took Papi's hands. He squeezed them and then he pulled me into a long hug.

He said, "You're a very brave girl." I started to cry into his shoulder. "You're very brave and no matter what happens I'm always going to be here for you." Papi hugged me for a long time and then he wiped some tears off my face.

"I should go to talk to your mami," he said.

My stomach gave three turns. Papi could tell I was nervous so before he went back to the bedroom, he made me a hot chocolate and put a blanket on my shoulders and told me to watch a movie, which he never lets me do in the morning unless I'm sick. Then he kissed my forehead and told me everything was going to be OK. I don't know what he meant by "OK" but I really hope he's right.

Te quiero mucho,
Lucia

Dear Tita,

I told Elisa about what happened and about how Papi is sleeping in a hotel now. Elisa could tell my heart felt tiny and crumpled and I know that she knows what that feels like.

I said, "I just wish I was someone else, not forever, just for now."

Elisa wrapped her arms around me but it didn't make me feel any better. "Why don't you sleep over tonight?" she said. I didn't really feel like it but I didn't want to hurt her feelings. I just shrugged.

"*Pleeeeaseeee,*" she said. "I'll take you on a nighttime adventure."

I didn't want to go on any adventures but I also didn't want to be in the apartment that felt empty with just me and Mami. So, I said yes and when I asked her, Mami did too.

Elisa's mami seemed to know I was sad because she wasn't moody at all, she was even extra nice. She made rice and chicken, which seems ordinary but there was something special about the way she made it. Her boyfriend Octavio ate with us too. I thought about how he wasn't Elisa's papi but that they still lived in the same house. Elisa seemed to be fine with that and that was sweet of her because I don't think I would like it one bit. After dinner, Elisa's mami made us do homework and even though she doesn't speak English she made us show her all of our work and explain what it was about. It seemed like we were teaching her things instead of her checking our homework. She said a lot of nice things about my homework and told Elisa, "Always be good to Lucia. I hope you are best friends for a long time."

I wondered if she had made that up right then and there, that Elisa and I are best friends. But really, I hoped that Elisa had told her. I liked the sound of it in the quiet apartment. For a moment it was just our breath and the water on the stove boiling for café con leche.

"Wow! Look it's snowing!" Elisa yelled and she ran to the window. Her mami and I followed. She gave me a look. I think it was full of special feelings of happiness for Elisa's first winter in New York and maybe sadness for all the ones they had not spent together. We all looked at the snow for some time. Even Octavio, who's a very quiet man, said, *qué lindo*. Then, Elisa's mami let me and Elisa have our own cup of coffee because she said we were becoming señoritas. The three of us sat together to drink it. Octavio drank his on the couch while watching TV shows in Spanish.

I thought Elisa had forgotten about the nighttime adventure, or maybe she had made it up to convince me to sleep over, or maybe she just wanted to distract me from Papi's mess. But Elisa didn't forget. I don't know why I was surprised.

Her mami made us go to bed early because her boyfriend has to get up early for work and she didn't want us making any noise. Elisa didn't argue, which I thought was strange, but I didn't say anything. Her mami tucked us into Elisa's little bed in the living room. As soon as her mami left, Elisa began to whisper. We were so close to each other, face to face, and I thought maybe this is what it's like to have a sister.

Elisa put her mouth right next to my ear and said, "We have to wait until Octavio starts snoring. That means they are both really asleep. Then I will show you something."

"What is it?" I whispered a little too loud. Elisa pressed her finger to my lips.

"It's a surprise."

Elisa and I waited for a long time. We put the covers over our heads so that her mami and Octavio wouldn't hear us. It felt like we were in a cocoon and there was no one else in the world. I started to get heavy and sleepy in cozy way.

"Do you think your mami and papi are going to get a divorce?" Elisa asked.

"Umm . . . I don't know," I replied because I realized I hadn't even thought about a divorce. I felt incredibly dumb.

"Maybe you'll get to have two apartments instead of one. That's kind of cool."

I know Elisa was trying to make me feel better by saying that but it didn't help. We were both quiet for some time and so many new questions popped into my mind: *Would I have to choose where to live? Would Papi move far away? Would Papi marry Anna? Would Mami ever find someone new?*

Elisa interrupted me, "Let's play a game until Octavio falls asleep?"

I nodded.

"I'll say a sentence to a story and then you have to say the next sentence. No matter what."

Our first story was about two girls who lived by themselves in a big forest in a little cabin. Elisa made them catch their own fish and kill a bear for winter coats. I made them make friends with the birds.

Elisa yawned. "That's enough for that one. Once upon a time, there was a girl in New York City named . . . Alicia and she was angry at the world."

"She had short blond hair and blue fire shot out of her eyes whenever anyone said anything she didn't like," I said and Elisa giggled.

"Nobody really liked her, but she was just misunderstood," Elisa continued.

"Really?" I said and Elisa nodded. "Alicia was misunderstood because she had a big secret."

Elisa closed her eyes.

"It's your turn," I said but she was too sleepy to reply.

I laid in the dark for some time. I thought about you and I wondered what you would say to make things better. That all of this would make me a stronger and more interesting person? I wasn't sure. Then I heard it, the very loud snoring coming from the bedroom.

"Wake up," I said. "You hear?"

"They're asleep?" Elisa whispered without opening her eyes.

"Yes."

She opened her eyes, "Be very quiet. Quieter than you have ever been in your life. If Mami catches us she will hit both of us."

I didn't think that was actually true, but I didn't want to find out. I tried to move as gracefully as a cat. Elisa took my hand and took me to the front door. I would have said that it was a bad idea to leave the apartment but since I couldn't make a sound, I just squeezed her hand hard. She didn't react. She turned the knob very carefully and my heart started to beat very fast since I don't like doing things that can get me in trouble. But it was too late. We were outside of the apartment.

Instead of going downstairs we went upstairs. We climbed floor after floor and I said, "Where are we going?" Elisa didn't answer. Finally, we stopped and she took a gold key out of her pocket. She opened a door and we walked out onto the roof. The wind rushed into our eyes and through Elisa's pj's, which we were both wearing. We started laughing.

"It's so pretty!" I said looking at all the little lights of windows shining in the dark and the big yellow moon hanging above us.

Elisa smiled big and her teeth looked sharp and bright in the dark. "No one is allowed up here," she said.

I was going to ask how she got the keys but I got distracted by the row of big trees with no leaves. Their branches stuck up in the air like lightning bolts.

"It's so cold!" I shouted up to the moon.

"And so beautiful!" Elisa shouted.

Elisa hugged me and I hugged her back, in part to stay warm, but also because she had taken me here so that I could be happy and she was saying without any words that she loved me very much. The city was sparkling around us and it felt like Mami and Papi's problems weren't the biggest thing in the world. It felt like there were lots of adventures waiting for me and Elisa. It felt like this was just the beginning.

Te quiero mucho,
Lucia

Alice

1

I live in Manhattan, on the Upper West Side, on the eleventh floor of an ancient building. Dad said that Billie Holiday practiced her songs on the seventh floor a long time ago. He would know because he's old and kind of a famous jazz musician. I don't know if you know who Billie Holiday is, but she's very important, and you should look her up. Mom is musician too, and a singer. But she stopped making new music after she had me. She says she's OK with that. I believe her because Mom can't lie. Dad, on the other hand, is a good liar. Mom says she forgives him for it because he has a lot of other "wonderful qualities." Like, name any instrument and Dad can play it. Play it really well. He's the best at the saxophone. Every summer he goes on tours in Europe and Japan and he plays his saxophone on big stages for old European and Japanese people. He says that when I'm older he will take me. But I don't really want to go to Europe. When he leaves it's just me and Mom and I like it that way.

Mom and I do everything together. I know that's weird because I'm eleven and I should have a kid best friend. For example, I know that the worst girl in the world, Lola, has a best friend Monique, and that the new girl Elisa is best friends with Lucia. I think Lucia likes Elisa because Elisa is really good at spelling and math and Lucia always gets the best grades. Lola likes Monique because they are both rich spoiled brats. No one really likes me because I'm weird. I thought I had a chance with the new girl because she seems pretty weird too. But Lucia got to her first and that's OK. It's OK because Mom is actually my best friend. Even when she's annoying and I hate her she's still my best friend. We watch movies together, we draw together, we have sleepovers when Dad is away, we eat mac and cheese and strawberries, we know the words to all the same songs. And I don't want that to change.

Sometimes I have dreams of someone taking Mom away or dreams of Mom disappearing. The dreams are coming to me more and more since we heard the bad news. In the dreams everyone is afraid of me and I'm not afraid of anything except not finding Mom. Sometimes I have to wake up and go check her bed. I stand over her just to make sure she's still breathing.

2

It's funny that Mom and I are best friends because we're really very different. First of all, we don't look anything alike. I have short blond hair and white pinkish skin. I have huge brown eyes, a crooked nose, and big sharp teeth. Mom has long wavy brown hair with some blond in it, a straight nose, and beautiful green eyes. Her skin isn't white or pinkish, it's what grown-ups call *olive-toned*. I love adventures, I have crazy thoughts and bad ideas, and I lie a lot. I like rollercoasters and the movies. Mom likes antique stores, our lake house, and libraries. She likes to stay at home, close the curtains, and to watch black and white movies. She likes it when it rains so she can sit next to the window and sip chamomile tea with honey while she looks out at the city. Sometimes I wonder what it would be like to have a kid best friend. Maybe if I were pretty and liked nice things like Mom I would have one. Elisa and Lucia send each other secret notes in class in Lucia's little purple notebook. I can't do that with Mom. They also take turns using Elisa's jump rope and seeing who can do the most jumps without messing up. Mom said she doesn't like to jump but that she would count for me. It's not the same. But Mom is good at other things. She's really good at playing pretend. She turns into an icy queen, a thief, a villain, and any animal in the world.

3

om picked me up from school today, which she hasn't done in a while since she's so tired all the time now. She seemed like she wasn't paying attention to what I said. I held her hand and it felt all small and squishy like a dead baby bird. She's been getting skinnier every month since the summer.

I said, "Mom what's wrong?" But she just shook her head and touched her hair the way she does when she's nervous.

We kept walking. I told her how the new girl, Elisa, well I guess she's not that new anymore, does this weird thing: she asks everyone for the juice boxes and chips they don't eat and takes them home in her backpack. Mom usually would have said something nice like, "It's good not to waste." But instead, she just kept nodding. I said that being the weirdest kid in class was *my* thing and it wasn't fair that Elisa was trying to be a weirdo by asking for chips and making drawings of evil cats and rats eating each other to death while Ms. Luz tried to teach us math. On a normal day Mom would have said something like, "Maybe you and Elisa could be friends." But she didn't say anything. She just looked up at the trees which are finally starting to fill up with little leaves again. Spring is Mom's favorite time of year.

In the elevator, I was about to ask Mom what was wrong again when our neighbor from the twelfth floor stuck his skateboard between the closing doors and stepped in. He was wearing Converse, white jeans, and a black-and-white striped t-shirt. No jacket. His jeans were covered in dirt and his forehead was sweaty and I could see a bloody scratch on his arm. His name is Story and he's a little older than me. Mom and I are always together when we see Story, and Story is always alone. Mom says he's very independent.

"Are you okay, Story?" Mom asked, finally acting like herself again. "Did you fall?"

Story mumbled, "I'm fine." I hoped Mom wouldn't ask any more questions. It was embarrassing.

"Well, if you need an ice pack or some band-aids just come knock on our door."

Story didn't even turn to look at us and I tried not to look at him, but I was too curious. Dad said his mom was a famous TV writer and that his dad "produced movies," whatever that means. He said that they were always traveling. The blood on his arm was still drying. It sparkled in the light. I decided I liked him, even though he seemed a little mean, and I hoped that he liked me back.

4

That night Mom and Dad said they needed to talk to me. I hate it when they say that. It usually means I'm in trouble. I was trying to think about what it could be about and since I've done a lot of not great things at school lately, I couldn't figure out which one they would be particularly upset about.

I was in my room working on my comic book. It's about a superhero who likes to wear boy clothes like me. She can melt anything with her laser eyes and flip over cars and ancient buildings. And she can tell when people are lying.

"I'm busy!" I called.

Mom said, "Alice, this is really important."

Mom and Dad sat on my bed. They seemed sad and serious and Dad was rubbing Mom's back and that made me want to run out of the apartment and take the elevator and keep running through the city until I tripped and broke my face.

"Look at me, sweetie," Mom said.

I didn't want to, but I did, and I saw that there were tears in her green eyes.

"Are you going to die?" I asked.

She looked at Dad. I could tell she was trying not to cry.

"No, sweetie. She's not going to die," Dad said, using his serious voice, but I wasn't sure if I believed him.

We had found out about Mom's cancer in August and it's

been non-stop doctor visits since. After each appointment things seem to get more and more complicated.

"Do they finally have a new liver?" I asked.

"That's the thing, there's been a delay."

"What? Why?"

Dad did the rest of the talking which felt blurry because something in my head wouldn't stop thumping. He said Mom had Hep C and that the doctors needed to get rid of that before putting in a new liver in and that was going to take some weeks and that Mom already started that treatment and that's why she was feeling sicker lately. The medicine to get rid of Hep C had all these horrible side effects. None of this made any sense. Why wouldn't the stupid doctors give Mom a fricking organ already? I plopped onto my bed next to Mom and Dad and screamed into my pillow. Then I started to cry. A big angry cry. They rubbed my back and tried to comfort me by saying things like, *We switched doctors, now it's Dr. B and she's the best in the city, which really means one of the best in the whole world.* But the only thing that would have made me feel better is if none of this was happening at all.

That night I couldn't sleep. I woke up all sweaty. I had one of those dreams where I lost Mom in the ocean, or in the library, or a museum, but I couldn't remember anything about it. All I had was a leftover bad feeling that something was terrible. Without turning the lights on, I changed clothes and then did something Mom and Dad really don't like. I opened up the window and sat on the fire escape with my legs hanging off the edge.

Way below I could see a homeless man sleeping in the alley. He used his backpack as a pillow. I wondered where his mom was. Did he ever visit her? Or did she already die? I really wanted to know so I said, "Hey! Excuse me sir . . ." But he didn't move and I didn't want to yell any louder so I just kept wondering about him and about a million and one other things. It was almost light outside again before I went back to bed.

5

At the kitchen table Mom said, "Your eyes are red. Did you sleep?"

I nodded and she kissed me on the forehead.

Mom, Dad, and I took a taxi to my school even though it's close by. They dropped me off and went to the hospital to take Mom to one of her million appointments. I fell asleep in my first class after putting my head on the desk. Elisa threw a paper at me so that I would wake up. She was trying to be nice so that I wouldn't get in trouble, but I turned back and said, "I'm going to cut your hand off." She looked confused. Lucia overheard and shot me a dirty look.

Ms. Luz told me to go to the nurse and I said, "But I'm not sick."

"I think you need a nap," she replied.

I called her the b-word. I thought I did it quietly but she heard and said, "Now you're going to the office."

Right then I felt like pulling her hair out and slapping her face. Because I HATE THE OFFICE. Mr. Mack, the principal, is SUCH A FAKE. He wears fancy suits and talks all smooth because he wants the rich parents to think he's cool.

Dad says Mr. Mack cares about cute little dinner parties and the big fat donations parents give to the school. On a normal day I would have just bit my tongue and let the metal taste fill my mouth. But this time after Mr. Mack gave me a speech I said, "Mr. Mack, you suck."

Mr. Mack called Mom but she didn't pick up. I knew she wouldn't. So he called Dad and he said he was talking to a doctor so he would call Mr. Mack back. Mr. Mack can't stand me so he called the school counselor. I waited for her in her lame office which had pictures of owls everywhere. There was even a stuffed toy owl on the couch. It was break time and I could hear the kids coming out of their classrooms. I started to get really sleepy again. I watched them walk past me. Some of them whispered to each other and laughed and laughed because they knew I had called Ms. Luz the b-word and that I was in big trouble. Elisa poked her head through the door.

"What are they going to do to you?" she asked. I could tell she felt kind of bad for me and that she didn't care that I said I was going to cut her hand off.

"Probably nothing," I said. Elisa didn't look so sure. She shrugged and said, "Good luck." Then she left to the cafeteria. What did she expect? I wondered what they did to kids at her last school in El Salvador. The counselor came into her office. She tried to talk to me but I gave her the silent treatment until I feel asleep on her scratchy green couch. I used her owl as a pillow. When I woke up she just sent me back to class like nothing had happened.

6

walked home from school alone. When Mom gave me permission to do this at the beginning of the year, I loved it. Today it felt lonely. And that lonely feeling got even worse when I saw Lola and Monique walking together and then Elisa and Lucia walking together too. I let out a big sigh and pretended not to care. I walked past them with my head up high like I had somewhere important to go.

Right when the elevator was about to close, Story walked in. It was the first it time it was just the two of us. "Hey," I said. Story just looked at me and gave me a nod. He made me feel nervous and excited. I wanted to say more but I couldn't think of anything good.

Back home Mom was lying down in the dark. Before she was sick she never did this. After we both walked back from school she'd cook up something healthy, but these days we order a lot of take-out. I sat on her bed and we ate sushi while we watched a black-and-white movie. I had homework, but Mom and Dad didn't tell me to do it, so I didn't.

I asked Mom, "Are you feeling side effects?"

She looked at me and mustered a small smile. "I just feel tired."

In the middle of the movie, she got up and I could hear her throwing up in the bathroom. I paused the movie because that's what she does when she goes to pee. Dad was in his studio. I opened the door and said, "Mom's puking."

He told me to keep watching the movie. I told him Mom would miss parts of it and he said it didn't matter.

"Of course it matters," I said.

"Alice, please, I've had enough of you today."

I went back to the bed but I didn't press play. I heard Mom throw up again. Then I heard Mom and Dad whispering in the bathroom.

"What are you talking about?!" I shouted but they didn't answer. I threw a pillow across the room and it landed in the hamper full of Mom's dirty clothes. She likes to wear things I would never wear: lavender, pink, silver, and light blue stuff, dresses and skirts. Mom came back with a little smile on her face.

"You waited," she said. Right then, as I put my head in her lap, I knew I made the right choice.

7

In the cafeteria, Elisa invited me to sit with her and Lucia. I faked like I had to think about it and then shrugged and followed her to a round table in the corner where other nice girls also sat. At first Lucia was quiet and seemed kind of afraid of me. Mom told me it's good to not always talk about yourself and to ask people questions, so I asked Lucia about her science project even though I really didn't care. Lucia said she was going to make a rain cloud appear in a jar.

"How are you gonna do that?" I asked, starting to get a little more interested.

"First, you put some drops of your favorite food coloring into water. Then you boil that water . . ."

But Lucia couldn't get very far because Lola interrupted. Lola is the worst girl in the whole school. But she thinks she's cool because she's a model and her mom's a model and her dad's a fashion designer.

"Alice, why do you have to be such a freak?" she asked.

The happiness that had built up in Lucia's face disappeared. "Just ignore her," she said in a quiet voice.

I didn't listen. I called Lola the c-word because it's the worst word I know and she's the worst girl I know. Elisa smiled a big smile that showed her teeth and Lucia frowned. Lola pinched my arm and I stood up and pushed her. Lola tried to kick me but failed. I kicked her back and didn't fail.

Lucia stood up and took three steps back. "Stop Alice! You're going to get in trouble." She looked really worried for me and I felt a kind of bad. Elisa shouted, "Fight!" A bunch of kids copied her and started chanting, "Fight, fight, fight!"

I kicked Lola right below her knee. She fell to the floor and screamed like a feral cat. She's a great actress. I didn't decide to do this, I swear, but all of a sudden I was on top of her pulling at her long blond hair. I wanted to see how it felt to pull it out of her head so I yanked harder and harder but not for long because I felt some big hands around my arms. It was Mr. Mack coming to Lola's rescue.

I yelled, "Get off me you creep!" I knew adults get very afraid when little girls call them that.

I was surprised to only get a warning. I think Mr. Mack was afraid I would call him a creep again if he got me suspended. He called Mom and Dad again because he wanted to say bad things about me, but neither of them picked up. I bit my tongue so I wouldn't laugh in his face.

"Go to class," he said, "I'll call them later." I could see his jaw get tight. He really hates me.

I walked home alone because Mom wasn't feeling good and Dad told Mr. Mack that he had to keep an eye on her. When I turned the corner, I saw Lucia and Elisa walking together again.

"Hey!" I shouted.

They both turned around at the same time. Lucia's eyes narrowed. Maybe she was scared of me all over again or maybe it was worse . . . maybe she just decided she didn't like me at all. Elisa grinned which made me feel a little better.

"Where are you guys going?" I asked.

"Lucia's apartment," Elisa replied.

Lucia poked Elisa in the ribs like she wasn't supposed to say that. I didn't understand why she was angry at me. Lola is a stuck-up idiot and I was really doing everyone a favor by taking her down. It was obvious that Lucia didn't even like Lola.

"Where do you live?" I asked.

"Broadway and 75th."

"Oh cool! We're super close. I'm on Amsterdam and 72nd."

"What did they do to you?" Elisa asked.

"Just a warning."

Lucia could've said something nice like, *let's walk together* but instead she grabbed Elisa hand and said, "Come on, my mom hates it when I'm late." They walked fast. Elisa turned back once and gave me a little smile. I think it said, *don't worry I don't hate you.* I still felt rotten. I wondered if Lola was right. Maybe I was a real freak and I would never have any friends. I got super sad for a second and I walked all slumped over looking at my dirty white combat boots stomping on the disgusting concrete. And then the sadness turned into this gigantic empty feeling.

When I got home Dad gave me a lecture about how absolutely unacceptable my behavior at school is and how dare I make things more difficult when everything is already so hard right now.

At the end he said, "Alice, you are going to a psychologist and . . . no movies for a week."

But then Dad must have forgotten. Or he probably was too tired to fight, because when he saw me in the bed cuddled up with Mom watching a movie just a little after the lecture he didn't say a thing. He just looked at us and sighed. Then he went to his studio and shut the door. Mom and I watched something funny and old. A handsome man was looking for a pretty lady in the rain. Then he found her and gave her a big smooch.

"What does it feel like to get kissed by a man?" I asked Mom.

She gave me a little smile. "Depends on the man . . . If you like him, it feels soft and warm. If you don't, it feels slimy."

I thought about all the boys in my grade and how stupid and gross they were.

I said, "How come all the boys I know are idiots?"

She thought for a second. I could tell she was getting sleepy and then she said with her eyes closed, "The boy upstairs . . . what's his name? Story? I like that name. He seems nice." Then she fell asleep and I paused the movie.

For a second, I thought about what it would be like to kiss Story but then I told myself all boys were gross and I would rather kiss the subway floor.

was sitting on the fire escape reading my Greek mythology book and eating watermelon. Every once in a while, I took breaks to see how far I could spit the seeds into the alley. I started thinking about what other kids from my class were doing. Was Elisa playing with her kitty named Kitty in the Bronx? Or maybe she was at Lucia's on Broadway and 75th? It made me a little sad to think of them hanging out without me. I got angry at Lucia because if it wasn't for her, Elisa and I would be friends. I thought about how it would be so much better if Lucia changed schools. I wished with all my heart that her parents would take her out of our school and put her into a private school. Then she could make a bunch of annoying stuck-up friends and forget all about Elisa.

I heard music coming from Story's apartment. Something old and goofy that Dad would probably know the name of and I thought I could hear Story humming along but I wasn't sure. I wondered if he was lonely like me and if other kids in his school thought he was weird.

Then Mom and Dad knocked on my door. They told me to come inside but I didn't want to. Dad rolled his eyes but Mom didn't care. She sat on the windowsill and stroked my short hair, which I cut myself.

"Is there more bad news?" I asked looking into the blue sky. I thought for a second what it would be like to jump from the fire escape into the alley. I saw myself break into chunks. My guts spilled onto the ground and the rats chewed on me. I thought about how that wouldn't be so bad. If it happened, I wouldn't have to hear any bad news, I would live inside a rat's stomach and turn into poop and then the bugs would eat me and I'd disappear.

Mom's voice was soft and weak, but she smiled. "It's good news. They have a liver for me."

I wondered why Mom and Dad weren't jumping with joy since we've been waiting for this for months. I looked into their faces. Mom was a pale skinny ghost. And Dad just looked older than ever with a deep new crease between his eyebrows. I was still.

"I'm going to have to be at the hospital for a while."

"How long?" I asked.

"Two weeks . . . if everything goes well." She touched my back. I moved away from her. Mom and I have never been apart. One time I tried to go to camp but I got sick on day two and Mom had to rent a car and come get me.

"If everything goes well?" I asked and my voice cracked.

"I shouldn't have said that. Everything is going to be alright . . . Dr. B said I'm still young and strong and that I'm going to be OK."

"Who the hell is this Dr. B?" I asked. "What the hell does he know?"

Dad cut in, "Hey! Language!"

Mom gently put her hand on his leg. "Dr. B, Dr. Bracamontes, is a she. She's one of the top oncologists in the whole nation. She's Lucia's mom."

My head started to throb. So now Lucia's mom was going to save my mom? I let out a long groan. I wondered if Lucia knew about Mom already or if she would find out. She might feel really sorry for me. *Poor Alice with a sick mom and no friends.* That would be worse that her hating me.

Mom kept talking: "Dad is going to be busy taking care of me, but you won't be alone. Aunt Marnie and Uncle Frank are going to come be with you."

All my thoughts of Lucia and what she did or didn't know completely disappeared. "WHAT?"

"I know they are not your favorite people, but they have very graciously offered their time. They're retired, their kids are grown-ups, and they're being very kind to us. I know Aunt Marnie is a little strict. But she's a wonderful person."

I kicked the bowl of watermelon down into the alley and watched it shatter. I remembered the homeless man the second after I did it and felt a little bit bad there would be glass in his sleeping spot.

Dad grabbed my arm hard and said, "Come inside."

"It was a mistake!" I yelled even though it wasn't.

I saw a head pop up from the window upstairs. I'm pretty sure it was Story looking down at the shattered bowl of watermelon which did make a pretty loud sound. Did he see me see him? I looked at Mom. She was touching her hair in that nervous way. I decided to be good. The three of us sat on my bed. I didn't want to cry but I started crying anyway and I curled into Mom's lap like a pet. I tried to think about what death meant. I thought of her body disappearing. All I could think about was a gigantic darkness that went on forever and forever. It was the loneliest feeling. I wanted to think of Mom getting better. For Mom to get better she needed to be cut open. She needed to be cut open by Lucia's mom. Because I didn't know what Lucia's mom looked like I saw Lucia instead, with her long black hair and her long skinny arms. She opened Mom with a pair of scissors and took out a big black moldy organ with her hands.

9

unt Marnie and Uncle Frank got here last night. Aunt Marnie has a round face, red cheeks, and a saggy belly. She always wears something with a cat on it. Yesterday it was a necklace with a white cat face on it. Its yellow eyes kept following me. She hugged Dad for a long time, Mom for a medium amount of time, and me for a very short time. I can't remember why she doesn't like me. Uncle Frank gave us all the same little squeeze. He's the opposite of Aunt Marie, a tall skeleton. And even though he's Dad's brother he's not really like him at all. He used to be a lawyer and he stayed in the same town upstate his whole life. He goes to church with Aunt Marnie every Sunday. He always wears a Yankees hat to hide that he's bald even though we all know it. I think he probably sleeps in it. Aunt Marnie does most of the talking and Uncle Frank also talks quite a bit, especially about baseball and the news once you get him going. But both of them talk really loud and I never remember anything they say. When they finally fell asleep, I could hear them both snoring in my room.

That night I slept in a cot in Mom and Dad's room. I didn't really sleep. I was half-asleep, half-awake. This time I saw Lucia digging through Mom's body and not finding the sick liver. Her arms got tired so she gave up and walked away. Mom's stomach crawled out of her body like an inch worm and escaped under the crack of the door. I wanted so badly to go to the fire escape and get some fresh air but it wasn't worth waking up Aunt Marnie and Uncle Frank. I went to the living room instead and put my forehead against the window.

There was Manhattan, all its little lights, all the other people who for some reason were awake too. For just a second I felt like Mom and I were tiny and didn't take up the whole world. I wanted to keep that feeling. I wanted to be as small as a button, no, smaller, as tiny as a fruit fly, or even better, I wanted to be a piece of sleep sand from a good night's rest. I wanted to feel like I didn't have a mom at all.

10

I woke up on the soft blue couch in the living room. Mom was touching my cheek.

"You didn't like the cot, Sugar?"

I put the pillow over my head. Everyone was already awake. I could hear Dad playing the piano in his studio. Something too fast. Something nervous.

"Go away," I said.

"That's no way to speak to your mother," Aunt Marnie called from the kitchen. I shot up from the couch and Mom gently put her hand over my mouth. She gave me a look that said, *Please don't, not today.*

The whole house smelled like bacon and honey. My mouth watered.

"I'm going to fatten you up!" Aunt Marnie called out.

I gave Mom a look and she smiled. "She's just trying to be nice," she whispered, and gave my hand a squeeze.

I went to my room and changed into a boy t-shirt, jean shorts, and my favorite red combat boots. Aunt Marnie's lip curled up. "I thought you went to a nice private school," she said. "Will they let you go in like that?"

Dad jumped in so I wouldn't say anything. "It's not a private school. It's a charter school. They don't have a uniform. The teachers are okay with the kids . . . expressing themselves."

Aunt Marnie peeked under the table to take a better look at my shorts while we served ourselves breakfast. Uncle Frank took his breakfast to the living room and turned on the news.

"It's a bad habit he has," she said shaking her head. "He watches the news in the morning and can't stop yapping about it all day."

I ate a bite of the eggs, all of the bacon, and some toast. Before Aunt Marnie could make a comment, I stood up and threw the rest away.

"Such delicious eggs, Aunt Marnie," I said when I sat down. She gave me a suspicious look.

In the taxi that Mom, Dad, and I took to school, I remembered a couple of reasons why Aunt Marnie doesn't like me. There was that one time I fed her precious cat Lulu a battery because I thought it needed energy, then that time I hid from her in the grocery store, and maybe the worst of all (and I *cannot* remember why I did this) the time I pooped in her closet. But wasn't I just a kid? Don't other kids do things like that? Don't I get a second chance? Aunt Marnie seemed like she already made up her mind about me.

When we got to school, Mom got out of the taxi to say goodbye. We hugged for a long time.

"I'm going to miss you so much," she said. "Promise you'll be a good girl?"

"I promise," I replied, but I crossed my fingers behind her back just in case.

11

In math class, I put my head on the desk. Lola, who unfortunately sits behind me, whispered, "What a weirdooo."

"Don't listen to her," Lucia told me. My face got hot and my fists clenched.

I lifted my head up. "Don't tell me what to do," I told Lucia. I immediately felt bad about that because I remembered it was her mom's job to save my mom's life. Shouldn't that make her less annoying? I think it actually did, but I didn't have time to debate that in my head because Lola made a snickering sound behind me. Time sped up. I grabbed my math textbook and hurled it at Lola's chest where her little boobies are growing. She let out sharp genuine gasp. I think this time I actually hurt her.

"OUCH!" she cried. I looked at her and there were real tears in her blue eyes.

I heard Elisa laugh, which made me happy for a second but then I saw Lucia beside me giving me a look . . . of pity? Like she was thinking *poor Alice, she can't even control herself if she wanted to.* That look made me feel like one of those gross jumbles of dust on the end of a used broom. I dropped back into my chair. This time I was really in trouble.

Ms. Lee told me I had to go to the office immediately. Soon I was sitting across Mr. Mack. He had his creepy long fingers with bitten nails on the telephone. He told me that this time I was suspended and that someone would have to come and pick me up at once. No matter what.

"I have your Aunt Marnie's number," he said with a little grin.

I said, "Please, please, *please,* Mr. Mack, I'm begging you, don't. Give me one more chance!"

He didn't. Of course. So, next thing I knew Aunt Marnie walked into the office. I could tell she was FURIOUS. Her cheeks were even redder than normal and she had sweat stains all around her armpits. But she gave Mr. Mack a big smile because she's a fake just like him. Mr. Mack said he wanted to speak to her alone. I waited outside next to a little table with books made by kids at my school. I looked through them and some were stupid but others were actually pretty good. I found one by Elisa. It was about an evil man called the Chicken King who liked to steal little girls and lock them in the tower of his castle. The Chicken King had a crown made out of leftover chicken bones and a red cape the color of blood. It was actually really good and scary. I thought it proved that Elisa and I should be friends. I wanted to read the ending of her story but Aunt Marnie walked out of Mr. Mack's office, looking a little less red but still red. She lectured me all the way home about how I was so lucky to be at such a nice school and that I was going to get myself kicked out if I didn't get my act together, blah, blah, blah. I bit my tongue so I wouldn't say anything. At least I was smart enough to do that.

12

When we got home Uncle Frank was watching a baseball game, he was yelling at the players like they could hear his advice. By then, Aunt Marnie was even sweatier than before and said she had to wash off.

"Don't you dare sit next to Uncle Frank," she said. "When I said no TV for a week, I meant it. That includes movies!"

Uncle Frank looked at me for less than a second. "What did ya do this time?"

"Lola Ferris called me a freak so I threw a book at her chest."

"Ha!" said Uncle Frank.

"It was a *textbook*," Aunt Marnie clarified from the bathroom. "Those things weigh 20 pounds. Alice could have really hurt her. I wouldn't be surprised if Lola's parents sue you." But Uncle Frank wasn't listening anymore. He was shouting at the little baseball players.

All of a sudden I hated everyone. I ran to my room and locked myself in there because I didn't want Aunt Marnie to see me cry. I wished Mom was next to me rubbing my back. I wished I was older and could live all by myself. I got the pillow all wet with hot tears. I thought about that disturbing Chicken King from Elisa's book; of all the little girls he took to his tower. Upstairs I could hear someone jumping. Maybe to music. I cried and cried until I fell asleep. A knock on my door woke me up. It was Uncle Frank.

"Hey kid," he said. "You OK?"

I shrugged.

"Your Aunt Marnie made lasagna," he said, giving me a couple big pats on the back because he knew in his head what I will never say out loud: Aunt Marnie probably makes the best lasagna in the world and I could never be too angry or sad to eat it. Her recipe is a secret, passed down from her great grandmother in Sicily. I made a deal with myself. I would eat the lasagna but I wouldn't look at her or talk to her the entire dinner.

During dinner Uncle Frank talked about what he always talked about: the news. I didn't listen because I felt like I couldn't listen to anything or anyone. But I saw Aunt Marnie shake her head and touch her cross and at one point she said, "God bless those children. How could anyone be so heartless, so horrible, to take them away from their mothers! Even if they are illegals . . ."

The phone rang and I stood up because I knew it was a call from the hospital. Uncle Frank picked it up first because he's fast when he wants to be. He turned his back to us and pressed the phone to his ear. "Aha . . . aha . . . aha . . ." he said and finally, "Well that's good." I wanted to push Uncle Frank over onto the floor just like I pushed Lola in the cafeteria but I couldn't move. My feet were stuck to the ground. He hung up.

"What is it?!" asked Aunt Marnie.

"There were some complications, but she's fine. The bad liver is out, the good liver is in. The worst part is over, Alice."

"Thank the lord for Dr. Bracamontes!" Aunt Marnie cried.

I could breathe again and this time I couldn't run to my room before the tears came. I started crying right onto my lasagna. I guess I made Aunt Marnie feel sorry for me because she got up and pressed me into her big stomach and started to pet me as if I were one of her cats. In any other situation I would have run away from her but I still felt stuck onto the ground.

Even though I don't believe in God I thanked something way bigger than me for saving Mom. I also sent a million invisible thank yous through the air to Dr. Bracamontes. I saw her as Lucia but older and in a white lab coat throwing away a disgusting glob into a trash can. I couldn't stop crying and Aunt Marnie wouldn't stop petting me.

"My poor sweetheart. Don't you worry, from now on everything is going to be just fine."

I wanted to believe Aunt Marnie. But I didn't.

13

The next morning Dad called me. I told him I wanted to talk to Mom but he said she was asleep.

"Why don't you wake her up?" I said. "She'll want to talk to me."

"She's not making much sense anyways, Alice. Her mind's a little crazy."

"What do you mean a little crazy?" I asked. "Forever?"

"No, not forever," he said. "Just for now. She's saying some weird things because the anesthesia hasn't completely left her body."

"Like what?"

"Like . . . earlier she told the nurse to get the goats out of the room."

"The goats?" I laughed and Dad laughed too.

Then Dad asked how it was going with Aunt Marnie and Uncle Frank and I almost told him everything, but instead I said, "Swimmingly," which is a word Mom likes to use. I knew if I told him Aunt Marnie wasn't letting me watch TV he would ask why. Then he would find out about Lola and the math textbook and how Elisa thought it was funny but no one else seemed to think so. But when I hung up, I wished I'd told him. My mind was tangled up in loops. And I had a feeling it was just going to get more and more tangled.

I sat on the fire escape to read my Greek mythology book. It was the first nice day in a long time. The sun on my body made me sleepy. I closed my eyes and thought about falling over into the alley where the homeless man slept. I wondered how long it would take Aunt Marnie and Uncle Frank to notice I was missing. I wondered if it I would die right away or just break my legs.

Upstairs someone was playing angry rock music. It must be Story, I thought. I stopped thinking about the homeless man and instead I thought about Story. Story with the green eyes, Story who took the elevator alone. I went into the living room where Aunt Marie and Uncle Frank sat on the soft blue couch watching a show about corny chefs who cry and yell at each other.

"Aunt Marnie," I said, trying to sound sure of myself. "I'm going to visit my friend upstairs."

She took a break from her stupid show to try to look into my brain. Maybe she could tell that I had no friends.

"I visit him all the time. Dad lets me."

She didn't seem convinced so I told her Story's parents were hippies and didn't own any technology and that's why Dad always let me go. Then she believed me. Aunt Marnie thinks a lot of people in Manhattan are hippies, which used to be true, but isn't true anymore. My heart was beating fast in the elevator because part of me thought Aunt Marnie would make me stay in my room and I didn't actually know what to say once I got to Story's apartment. What if he hated me like everyone else at school? I gave his door the lightest knock and was about to turn around, but he opened it.

We stood in front of each other. He was older than me but

I was a little taller. I looked at his green eyes, his wavy black hair which went down to his shoulders, a shirt with Japanese writing on it, and a beautiful diamond necklace which seemed like it was his mom's. I thought he looked pretty and that he was probably one of the popular kids at his school. I was happy that he had no idea who I was.

"I'm your neighbor," I said. "Alice."

He told me his name and I pretended like I didn't already know it. I told him my Aunt Marnie sucked and that I was bored. He nodded and said I could come in. I followed him into his apartment which was much bigger than ours. I remembered Dad said his parents rented the whole floor which was an extremely expensive thing to do.

"Where are your parents?" I asked.

Story didn't answer. We walked past his living room where everything was black and white, even the big silent dog that sat on the couch. Then we went down a dark cool hallway. There was a painting on the wall with thick blue brushstrokes and pieces of green glass sticking out of it. At first, I thought it was a painting of nothing and then I thought it was actually a painting of a bad dream and I wondered why someone would want a big bad dream on their wall.

"Why is it so dark in your house?" I asked.

Story didn't answer. We were inside of his room and he closed the door.

14

I liked Story's room because it didn't seem like a kid's room. It seemed like a room for a teenager and I want to be a teenager soon so I can do whatever I want. When I was in there, I completely forgot about Aunt Marnie and her stupid rules and feeling lonely.

Story's room looked expensive like the rest of his house. He had lots of windows but kept the curtains closed besides the one near the fire escape. He had a big TV, an Xbox, a wall decorated with skateboards, and an electric guitar. I had a feeling he was one of those kids who my Dad likes to call "a spoiled brat."

"Wanna see something?" Story asked, and I nodded. I thought he was going to show me how he could kill people in his video game, which I would have liked, but he showed me something else. He took it out of his pocket: a shiny silver square with a gold eagle on it. With one quick movement he flipped it open, and like magic a little fire danced on it.

"Wow, that's cool," I said and meant it. I had never seen a lighter like that before.

"It's a Zippo. It was my grandpa's when he was a soldier in World War II. He just died."

"Why did you get to have it?" I asked, because it seemed like the kind of special thing a grown-up keeps in his drawer, not the type of thing a twelve-year-old carries around in his pocket.

"Because I was his favorite and when he was sick with cancer, he gave it to me."

The word cancer made the room feel smaller.

"My mom has cancer," I said.

"I hope she doesn't die from it like my grandpa," he said in a soft low voice and I felt like he actually meant it.

He went over to his desk where he had some superhero toys. I call them toys, but Dad says they are actually overpriced "collectibles" and that's why he never buys me any. Story picked up a Superman toy and started to melt off his perfect little face. I laughed. A strange smell came out of the peach-colored plastic as it turned black. It me made a little dizzy. Story opened his window a little wider. I didn't want Aunt Marnie to give me a big boring speech so I left after we finished melting Superman's muscly chest.

Right before I left, Story said, "Come over tomorrow."

For the first time in a long time, I think I actually felt great. I wondered what kind of things Elisa and Lucia did together. I could imagine Elisa liking to burn things but not Lucia. I thought that the best thing in the world would be if Elisa, Story, and I could be friends. Maybe I would tell her about him. Maybe I would invite her over and introduce them. Would she also ask Lucia to come? All of a sudden it seemed too complicated. Lucia was too different from us. Too good.

15

The great feeling didn't last very long. Once I got back to the apartment and sat down for dinner with Aunt Marnie and Uncle Frank I started to feel prickly again like I could have stood on top of the table and kicked things off onto the floor, one by one. But I didn't want to get into any more trouble because I thought Aunt Marnie might not let me go visit Story. So instead, I turned Aunt Marnie into one of the toys in Story's room. She had mini cat earrings, mini red cheeks, a mini double chin. I held Story's Zippo to her red cheeks and they got droopy and her eyes mixed into her nose and I smiled a little as I ate the leftover lasagna.

"Why do you have that smirk on your face?" Aunt Marnie asked.

"Your face is all mixed up."

She rolled her eyes at me and then looked at Uncle Frank. But he had more important things to talk about. He started to tell us again about the president and the children he put in cages.

"Again, Frank?" said Aunt Marnie. "This is not dinner conversation." But you can never stop Uncle Frank once he starts talking about politics. He talked about the violence and war in Central America. He talked about children and mothers and fathers who walked and walked and walked to get away from it. He talked about them coming to the United States and then not being able to get in. He talked about the children being taken away from their moms and dads and being put into little jails, *like dogs*, he said, *like apes!* It made me think about Elisa. She's from El Salvador. I wondered if they ever put her in a cage. And because once you start to think of one bad thing, you start to think about everything bad, I thought of Mom dying. I thought about not being able to see her ever again.

"I'll pray for them tonight," said Aunt Marnie. It was my turn to roll my eyes at her and she snapped back, "You better fix that face of yours, missy!"

I said, "At least I have a face!" which must have sounded strange to someone who hadn't seen Aunt Marnie burning in my imagination, but Uncle Frank seemed to understand because he went, "Ha!"

I got up and washed my plate because I was sick of both of them and sick of hearing about the poor kids and the cruel world. I went to my room and made up a new superhero. His name is Poem and he can shoot fire out of his hands and melt away all the cages.

16

When I come home from school, Aunt Marnie forces me to do my homework. I don't get dinner unless I do it. Well, I only get a piece of toast. And it's awful to eat toast in your room when you smell meatballs in the kitchen. Dad said I'll probably get fat living with Aunt Marnie. Uncle Frank says that's good because I'm skinny as a rod. Mom doesn't say anything. She is usually asleep. The doctors said she's still very sick. Anyway, the point is now I do my homework right away, which actually isn't that bad, because afterwards if Story isn't at karate class, or shopping with his mom, or eating out with his dad, I get to hang out with him.

Yesterday when I knocked on his door, the first thing Story asked is if he could have my shirt.

"Absolutely not," I said. It was my dad's shirt from a music tour he did in 1976. It had a naked woman on it with a skull in the middle of her boobs. She had a calm face and beautiful long hair.

"What do you want for it?"

I said, "Your Zippo."

Story smiled and said, "Never." But then he thought for a second. "What if I give you $100? You can buy a Zippo with that."

"Where are you going to get $100?" I asked.

Story didn't answer. I followed him to his parent's room, into his mother's closet. He opened her underwear drawer and inside there was an envelope with more money than I had ever seen in my life. He took out a bill and handed it to me.

I felt a little bad sticking the bill into my pocket because it wasn't really my shirt I was selling, but I told myself Dad would probably never notice. He's gone on a million tours. Besides, I liked the way it felt to stick money into my pocket. He took off his shirt. I thought a second before I took off mine and then realized it didn't really matter. Our bodies looked pretty similar, too skinny and pale, and my chest is basically still flat like boy's. So, I pulled off the shirt without even turning my back to him. Story smiled. Then we traded. Now I had a shirt with pigeon on it with a question mark on top of its head and Story wore the beautiful lady. I felt like maybe this was the type of thing Elisa and Lucia did. Not selling, but trading clothes?

Story and I began to burn the orchid by the window. First just the white edges turned black and then the fire ate each petal until it turned into soft ash. We played with the ashes. I said they felt like a baby's eyelid and Story said they felt like his mom's rabbit coat.

"Won't you get in trouble?" I asked.

Story shook his head no.

When I got downstairs, Aunt Marnie gave me a nasty look. "Why do you have a black smudge on your face?" I pinched my arm to punish myself. I thought I had cleaned everything up. Her eyes went up and down and all around me.

"Story and I were drawing . . . with . . . charcoal."

"What is that silly shirt you have on?" she asked. I pinched myself harder.

"This shirt?"

"Yes, that ridiculous shirt, with the pigeon. Is that shirt yours? I've never seen it."

I started to walk to my room before she figured out the truth, but she put her hand on my shoulder.

"No, you stop right there. You had on your father's shirt. I remember now because I thought it was obscene."

"No, I didn't!" I yelled, because I hated Aunt Marnie's chubby little fingers on me. If I were really brave, I would've bit them, but instead I called her the b-word. Aunt Marnie turned different colors. First white, then pink, then red, and I wondered if she would pop and explode all over everything. I knew something really bad was about to happen.

I stomped to my room and I slammed the door in Aunt Marnie's face. She came in, grabbed my ear, and twisted it.

"OUCH!" I yelled. I was shocked. A grown-up had never hurt me before.

"I'm going to call the police on you!"

Aunt Marnie let go. "Go right ahead, dear," she snarled. "Let's see if they believe a word you say, you little liar . . . And let me tell you one thing, no more of this Story kid. He's a bad influence."

"I'm calling the POLICE ON YOU," I said again, because grown-ups are very afraid of the police.

"What's that racket?!" called Uncle Frank over the news blasting in the living room.

But Aunt Marnie didn't stop, "NO more Story. You get it? And no more swearing, no more *losing* your father's shirts, no more rolling your eyes, no more smirking, no more lying. I'm going to take the brat out of you, missy. You get it?"

Then it was her turn to slam the door on me.

17

When she left, I cried and cried into my pillow. I thought about a lot of things: the orchid burning in Story's room, how it turned into little bits of black that flew in the air for just a millisecond. The ashes made me think of flies that only live for a day. I wished I was one of them. Then I would fly around, suck on some trash, and die. I wouldn't even have time to think of Mom, or Aunt Marnie, or Lola Ferris, or Dr. Bracamontes . . . I screamed into the pillow until my throat hurt. It made me feel a little better but I still had lightning bolts going through my body and needed to do something else.

I went to the fire escape and let my legs swing in the air. I thought about leaving forever. I could take a backpack with favorite comic books, my notebook, my markers, and the $100 I got for Dad's shirt. But then I looked down at the alley and thought about the homeless man sleeping with his backpack as a pillow and that didn't seem comfy at all. So instead of looking down I looked up into the evening sky. Electric blue and a little warm with the summer tucked into it. I could hear Story singing over his rock music and I thought why not climb the fire escape and visit him?

had never climbed the fire escape before and it was scary when I looked down at my striped socks on the thin metal ladder. The alley was really far down and all of a sudden I really didn't want to fall. I looked back up again and followed Story's voice. His window was open and I peeked my head through. Story stopped singing and his green eyes got twice the size.

"I'm sorry," I said immediately. I was embarrassed and looked down again, which made me super dizzy. I looked back up. "Did you know our rooms are right on top of each other?"

He shook his head because I think I scared him so much he didn't have any more words left in him.

"Do you want to see my room?" I asked. He was quiet. "Aunt Marnie said I can never see you again because you are a bad influence. If she sees you, she will actually kill me and she might kill you."

"OK, I'll come see your room," said Story.

We went down the ladder together. First me and then Story. A quick flashing image came to me. Story falling on top of me and both of us falling down ten floors. Both of us dead. But instead, we were standing in my room. My walls are coral pink because that's the color my mom painted them when I was a baby. Story looked strange surrounded by them since he was dressed in all black. His eyes went over my superhero posters, the pictures of me and Mom I stuck to the back of my door, the notebooks on my desk, my colored pencils and markers. I wanted to know what Story thought, but he didn't say anything and I didn't ask him. He took out his Zippo and flipped it open. The fire swayed between his fingers.

"Is there anything your aunt gave you?" he asked.

Aunt Marnie had really never given me anything. Not even for my birthday or Christmas. I shook my head.

"What about something she really likes?"

I remembered her stupid necklace which she left on the dining room table. The one with the big white cat in the middle. I remembered how its yellow eyes watched me on the first day she arrived.

"Stay here," I told Story. "Don't make a sound."

I tiptoed down the hallway. I could hear Aunt Marnie watching a soap opera in Mom's room and Uncle Frank watching news in the living room. I snatched the cat necklace and put it under my new shirt, Story's old shirt. My hands were shaking a little when I did it. I tiptoed back into my room and closed the door so very quietly.

"Maybe we shouldn't do this," I whispered to Story as I handed him the necklace.

"Fine," he said. "I'll just got back to my room." He even started to go out the window and I should've let him leave but instead I said, "Wait. Where are you going?"

"Yes, or no?" Story asked. I thought of Elisa and Lucia. Did they still play with dolls? Did they read books to each other? Did they braid each other's long hair or make each other bracelets? I wanted to know. But whatever it was I was almost sure they didn't do bad things like me and Story. I also thought I might never know because they would never invite me to play with them. Really at that moment, Story felt like my only friend in the whole world and the last thing I wanted was for him to leave.

"OK. Let's do it," I said.

Story smiled. He took out the Zippo and put it to the cat's face. He held it there for a while but it wouldn't catch on fire.

"Do you have nail polish remover?" he asked.

I said yes and tiptoed to the bathroom. Underneath the sink I found mom's nail polish remover and all of her favorite colors, light blue, coral, silver. My eyes filled with tears and my throat burnt, but I bit my tongue because I didn't want Story to think I was a baby. I looked at myself in the mirror. I saw circles under my eyes. *Do normal kids have those? Do I look like a freak?* I wondered.

Back in the room I gave Story the nail polish remover. I said, "Let's do it near the window. I don't want it to smell."

We sat on the windowsill next to the curtains that danced in the night breeze. Story poured a little nail polish remover on the cat's face and tried to light it but it didn't catch. So, I poured a little more and it still didn't light. We took turns pouring and lighting passing the cat back and forth. And then finally when the necklace was in Story's hands and the Zippo in mine, the white face and yellow eyes caught on fire. Story and I started giggling. I covered his mouth so that Aunt Marnie wouldn't hear him and just as I did the curtain blew in a little deeper into my room, a little closer to Story, and I saw it happen the way you see awful things happen, in slow-mo. The burning cat touched the curtain and the curtain caught on fire. The fire climbed up the fabric like a wicked spider. My mouth opened and I couldn't close it. I watched the fabric Mom chose years ago, all those pink and yellow flowers, get eaten up and turn black but also into little bits of red and orange that flew into the air like evil wings. It was one of those that landed on my vintage Batman poster.

It was really amazing how quickly the fire chewed things up. How quickly it spread. I had never seen anything so incredible. I think I was so impressed that I couldn't move or feel anything but awe. I don't know what Story was feeling but I think I saw a little smile on his face. Soon my favorite poster of the Joker was turning black. Long strips of bright orange flames reached out of it and attacked the new drawings I had just made and taped onto the wall. Bits of paper still on fire fell on top of a pile of clothes I left on the floor and that caught on fire too. The whole room started to fill with smoke. I think that's when Story stopped smiling because we both started to cough and we couldn't stop.

Aunt Marnie and Uncle Frank burst into the room. Aunt Marnie started to scream her head off.

"YOU ARE THE DEVIL!" she yelled at me over and over again. Her eyes were bulging out of her face. Uncle Frank didn't say anything he just ran away out of my bedroom, down the hall, out the back door, and he started to make his way down the ten flights of stairs. Aunt Marnie grabbed my wrists and Story's and even though you are not supposed to when there is a fire, we took the elevator because Aunt Marnie would have fainted trying to go down like Uncle Frank did. Part of me hoped the three of us would get stuck in the elevator and just burn up once and for all. But we didn't and the elevator took us down to the street.

There was Sonia from the ninth floor who gives acting classes to famous people, her sister Lorena whose only job is to walk the poodle that was in her arms, the annoying brothers who play basketball inside the apartment, the retired ballerina with her ancient husband in his wheelchair, and next to them, a very beautiful thin woman with green eyes just like Story's. She looked extremely nervous and then extremely relieved when Story ran into her arms. As soon as they ended their embrace, they both looked up at the eleventh floor. My apartment. I tried to make eye contact with Story, but he wouldn't look at me. It was like if I never existed.

Aunt Marnie and Uncle Frank, who probably wanted nothing to do with me, stood behind me. I wondered if I should try to run off before the fire fighters and police came. Would they try to stop me? I didn't want to answer any questions. I didn't want to go to juvie! Wasn't all of it my fault? I was almost about to make a run for it even if Uncle Frank would dart behind me. I'd decided I probably could outrun him. But then I felt a tap on my shoulder. It was Lucia.

"Hey Alice, what's going on?" she asked. We were both silent for some time while I was still deciding to either stay or run away forever. I thought it would be better to run away since no one would ever want to be with me after what I'd done. I thought about the homeless man. I thought that at least Mom would really miss me.

"My apartment is burning," I answered.

"Oh . . ."

We stood there together watching. Huge ugly clouds of smoke poured out my window. People in the crowd started to take pictures and videos. I felt like yelling at them, but my body was becoming very weak and my thoughts didn't make any sense anymore. They were spinning around in my brain and bumping into each other.

"Where's your mom and dad?" she asked.

I answered like a zombie: "They're in the hospital. My mom has cancer. Your mom did her liver transplant."

Lucia looked surprised. I guess she didn't know about Mom and her cancer. The sirens got louder and louder and I got dizzier and dizzier.

"I'm sorry your apartment is on fire," she said, kind of loud so I could hear her, "and that your mom has cancer . . ." Her eyes had gotten soft. She put her hand on my shoulder.

"Thanks," I said knowing that I wouldn't be able to stand up much longer.

"If you need books or clothes or anything, you can come over. You know we're like practically neighbors."

The firefighters parked their huge trucks and rose up and up into the sky in little white boxes. They stopped to spray water into my room, onto all the burnt photos of me and my mom, my comics, my drawings, my three pairs of combat boots, Story's t-shirt with the pigeon on it, my book of Greek mythology . . . All destroyed. How was I going to explain any of this to anyone? The water shattered some of the windows and little pieces of glass fell down like stars. The crowd went, "Ohhhh!" The fire was shrinking. Lucia, who I forgot was still next me, started to jump and clap. All the neighbors joined her cheering and that's when I fainted.

When I woke up, I was surrounded by Aunt Marnie, Uncle Frank, Lucia, and Dr. Bracamontes.

Aunt Marnie was blessing herself. "Thank the heavens!" she cried.

Uncle Frank was grabbing my hands. "C'mon, kid. Stand up."

"Hold on," said Dr. Bracamontes. "Let's let her just sit up for a bit."

But Uncle Frank kept pulling at my arms.

115

"Listen to the doctor, Frank! This is the woman who saved Daria's life! She knows what she's doing."

Uncle Frank let go and I sunk back into the cement.

I looked at each one of them and I saw something unexpected in their eyes. Aunt Marnie didn't seem like she wanted to kill me. Uncle Frank was actually looking at me, really looking. Dr. Bracamontes' eyes were kind and peaceful. They told me that I was going to be fine. And Lucia wasn't giving me that annoyed look that she gives me when we are at school. Nobody wanted me to run away or disappear forever. Uncle Frank, Lucia, Dr. Bracamontes, and even Aunt Marnie were all worried about me. I didn't think I deserved any of their caring feelings but I did let their kindness wrap around my heart which was hurting so much.

I looked down at the dirty pavement and started to cry. They weren't all sad tears. They were more complicated. I think, as Mom would say when she cries for seemingly no reason, I felt "deeply touched." I cried and cried. I saw the tears fall onto the warm cement and turn glittery. I think Lucia saw them too. She took hold of my hand and I squeezed back.

●   ●   ●

Dear Tita,

I haven't written to you in a long time. It's not that I haven't
been writing. I actually started to write new things, poems,
stories, and the beginning of books. I never showed my letters
to you to anyone else, but I have shown my other writing to
Mami, Papi, Elisa, and Alice, and they say I'm really good
and that makes me happy. The hardest thing to write is a
poem. Papi likes poems better than stories and novels. Papi
told me that if you are a really good poet, you could fit a
whole life into a poem. He said most novels are a waste of
time. I don't know if I believe him but it did make me stop
and think. Right now, I'm writing a long story about Elisa.
Sometimes, and only when I ask, she tells me bit and pieces
from her journey from El Salvador to the United States. She
told me she walked in a group. They walked so much her feet
got blisters all over. When I winced, she assured me they also
took buses and one time they all sat on top of a train. She
told me that she spent a lot of time in my country and that
most of the Mexicans treated her nice. They gave her pesos
when she asked for it. Tamales and tortas for free. But some
of them weren't nice at all. I never get a lot of details and I
don't ask for more because her voice always gets sad and low
when she remembers. So, I'm writing in the gaps. She doesn't

know I'm writing it. I don't really know if I'm ever going to tell her. You never know how Elisa will react to things.

But this morning I feel like writing about Mami and Papi again.

Without Papi coming home late and lying to Mami all the time, she started to act different. She started coming home from work earlier. After dinner she always wanted to go on a walk and keep talking to me. Then one day on one of our walks she said, "Shouldn't we get a dog?" And I said YES! So now we have a chihuahua, just like you used to have. Her name is Lupe. Even though I miss my old life sometimes, I'm happy living in the apartment with just Mami, Lupe, and me.

Papi is different too. I see him on Mondays and Wednesdays after school and on Saturdays. I still can't put my finger on exactly how he's different. At first, just right after the whole truth came out, he seemed a little afraid of me. He was extra careful and sweet. It made me a little nauseous, like eating a cake with too must frosting on it. After a couple of days, I couldn't handle it! I said, "Papi, can you just be yourself and not a weird prince?" He laughed and laughed and said, "OK, mi corazón." And he really did keep his word. Now he's himself but less sneaky and when we hang out together, I don't have to be worrying about the texts he's getting.

Elisa is still my best friend. She's still a little crazy and that's one of the things I like about her. She makes me think about things I would never normally think about and do things I would never do. For example, the other day she asked me if Papi could take us to the Statue of Liberty. I realized I had never seen the statue up close. I thought I knew about her because she's so famous, but actually I didn't know about her at all. Did you know her crown has seven spikes to represent the seven continents? On the ferry, Elisa's ponytails were flying in the wind and she was smiling the biggest smile I'd ever seen. It was impossible not to smile with her. Even Papi couldn't help but pat her on the head.

Alice is my friend now too. *Alice.* We became friends in the strangest way. One evening Mami, Lupe, and I were going out on one of our walks and we saw a building on fire. Not the whole thing. The flames and the smoke were coming out from a room on one of the floors near the top. That's when I bumped into Alice and I asked her what was going on. She told me it was her apartment that was burning up. It made her feel so terrible that she fainted! Right in front of me. Mami helped her wake up by putting her legs over her lap so that the blood could flow to her heart. We stayed with Alice until her dad came. Mami had his phone number because she's Alice's mom's surgeon. Alice was really sweet while she was waiting with us. She said thank you to Mami for saving her mom's life and pet Lupe in a nice way. Lupe seemed to know Alice was sad because she sat in her lap and gave her lots of kisses like I'd never seen her do with any other stranger.

After the fire, Alice changed. She missed school for a few days. When she came back, I saw her sitting alone at lunch. I asked her if she wanted to sit with me and Elisa. It seemed sad that she would have to eat all by herself after a horrible fire and her mom almost dying. I started to see that Alice is actually really funny and even nice when she's in a good mood. When she's in a bad mood Elisa and I have learned to leave Alice alone. Then she sits down by herself and reads one of her comic books, and that's OK. Sometimes Alice and Elisa decide to play tag with the boys, which I don't like. But Mami says that's there's nothing wrong with that and that I should be comfortable with change because nothing ever stays the same.

I said, "Nothing . . . nothing at all?"

And Mami smiled. "Well, except one thing."

"What?"

"My love for you."

I was quiet for a while because I was afraid to ask my next question. *But what about when you die?* We were sitting on the train. Mami put her arms around me and drew me in close. Then like if she read my mind she said, "I still feel Tita's love. It's a gift I get to keep forever. When I'm sad, I let it wrap around me like a warm blanket. When I'm happy I let it shine out of me." I leaned my head on Mami shoulder. I believed what she said and it made my heart peaceful.

I hope you liked my update.

Te quiero hoy y siempre,
Lucia

ACKNOWLEDGMENTS

I wish to thank the many people who supported me and helped to bring *City Girls* into the world.

LAUREN BLODGETT, director and founder of The Brave House: Without you this book wouldn't exist. Thank you for giving me the idea of writing Elisa's story, for our brainstorming sessions after a long day of work, and for connecting me to Turkey Land Cove and Marina. Your unwavering belief in me and this story helped me believe in my ability to write it.

MARINA BUDHOS, author and editor: Thank you guiding me and dedicating hours of your time to *City Girls* when I was a complete stranger. You helped me structure this book, understand what it means to write for children, and not get discouraged along the way. Conversations with you were absolutely pivotal.

HAL NIEDZVIECKI, author: Thank you for listening to my pitch and for connecting me with Seven Stories. I don't know if you understand how much your kindness changed my life.

RUTH WEINER, publisher of Triangle Square Books for Young Readers and publicity director of Seven Stories Press: Thank you for reading my query, for reading my manuscript, and for trusting in my vision. It has been a dream come true.

OONA HOLAHAN, assistant editor at Seven Stories: Thank you for your insightful and precise edits, for your gentleness and honesty.

TESS WEITZNER, my agent: Thank you for advocating and listening and giving me hope and confidence. Your patience and positivity safeguarded this process.

MICHAEL IVES and DOUG PARKER: My favorite professors, thank you for teaching me how to ask interesting questions and how to find joy, risk, and wonder in writing. You helped me know I wanted to be a reader and a writer.

NICK and MY MOM: Thank you for reading draft after draft of *City Girls*, for challenging me with your questions, listening to all of my ideas, and telling me what you really think. For taking my dreams seriously and loving me no matter what.

RUBY and DEE: Thank you for inspiring me, sharing your story, and letting me ask you hard questions. I feel so blessed you are in my life.

PAPI: Gracias por ser tú, por enseñarme que ser artista es algo natural, casi imposible de no hacer, que es algo que le das amor y atención todos los días de tu vida, que es parte de la rutina, nada fuera de lo ordinario.